"I see no reason ~~why~~ be raised like the child of a prince it is."

"Then I have some deliciously good news for you," Zeus informed her with a little bow. "Assuming this isn't all an elaborate ruse that will be uncovered shortly by the palace's medical staff, allow me to be the first to congratulate you."

"Why?" she asked, suspicion stamped all over her. "For what?"

Zeus only gazed down at her, that temper still curling around inside him.

"On your nuptials."

"My...what?"

"Oh, happy day," Zeus said, letting his voice carry and rebound back from the pristine walls like so much dizzy heat. "We are to be married, little hen. You lucky thing. Women have been jostling for that position since before I was born."

"Not me!" She looked almost insultingly horrified. "I don't want to marry *you*!"

Which, he could admit, was another reason she was perfect. Zeus could not have tolerated any of the women who did actually want to marry him. They longed for either the man they thought he was or the throne he would take, and either way, it wasn't him.

Only this woman, only Nina, would do.

Pregnant Princesses

When passionate nights lead to unexpected heirs!

Vincenzo, Rafael, Zeus and Jahangir are princes bound for life by their ruthless quests to rebel against their tyrannical fathers. But their plans will be outrageously upended when forbidden nights with forbidden princesses leave them facing the most shocking of consequences...and convenient marriages that spark much more than scandal!

Read Vincenzo and Eloise's story in
Crowned for His Christmas Baby
by Maisey Yates

Read Rafael and Amalia's story in
Pregnant by the Wrong Prince
by Jackie Ashenden

Read Zeus and Nina's story in
The Scandal That Made Her His Queen
by Caitlin Crews

And look out for
His Bride with Two Royal Secrets
by Marcella Bell

Coming soon!

Caitlin Crews

THE SCANDAL THAT MADE HER HIS QUEEN

H HARLEQUIN®
PRESENTS®

Recycling programs
for this product may
not exist in your area.

ISBN-13: 978-1-335-56931-8

The Scandal That Made Her His Queen

Copyright © 2022 by Caitlin Crews

This edition published by arrangement with Harlequin Books S.A.

For questions and comments about the quality of this book,
please contact us at CustomerService@Harlequin.com.

Harlequin Enterprises ULC
22 Adelaide St. West, 41st Floor
Toronto, Ontario M5H 4E3, Canada
www.Harlequin.com

Printed in U.S.A.

USA TODAY bestselling, RITA® Award–nominated and critically acclaimed author **Caitlin Crews** has written more than one hundred books and counting. She has a master's and PhD in English literature, thinks everyone should read more category romance and is always available to discuss her beloved alpha heroes. Just ask. She lives in the Pacific Northwest with her comic book artist husband, is always planning her next trip and will never, ever, read all the books in her to-be-read pile. Thank goodness.

Books by Caitlin Crews

Harlequin Presents

Chosen for His Desert Throne
The Sicilian's Forgotten Wife
The Bride He Stole for Christmas

Royal Christmas Weddings

Christmas in the King's Bed
His Scandalous Christmas Princess

Rich, Ruthless & Greek

The Secret That Can't Be Hidden
Her Deal with the Greek Devil

Visit the Author Profile page
at Harlequin.com for more titles.

For Nina Pépin, because she asked

CHAPTER ONE

CASTLES AND PALACES and all such trappings
of royalty, Nina Graine reflected dryly, were
much better in theory than in practice.

She would know, having had far too much
of that practice.

In theory, castles were all about fairy tales.
She'd thought so herself while growing up in
the orphanage. Think of castles and it was all
happy, merry songs dancing gracefully on
a sweet breeze. Happy-ever-afters sounding
from on high, possibly with the help of fleets
of cantering unicorns.

Nina was pretty sure she'd had that dream
at least a thousand times.

But then she'd learned the truth.

In practice, castles were dark and drafty
old things. Most of them had been fortresses
first and were therefore built in places where

ransacking armies and the odd barbarian could be turned away with a minimum of fuss. They were filled with musty tapestries and bristling with trophies of battles past. No matter how modernized they claimed to be, there were always too many ghosts in the fortified walls.

Palaces, meanwhile, were less about defense and more about drama. *Look at me*, a palace cried. *I'm better than everything and especially you.*

Like the one she was currently visiting in the island kingdom of Theosia, sitting pretty in the Mediterranean Sea. The Kings of Theosia had called this place the Palace of the Gods, clearly not suffering from any form of impostor syndrome.

She *almost* started thinking about the palace's current occupants, the unwell, old King Cronos and his only son and heir, the wicked, scandalous, upsettingly beautiful Prince Zeus. *Almost.*

But there would be time enough for that.

Instead, Nina focused her attention on the stuffy little room she'd been left in. It could have been in any palace, an afterthought of a space tucked away in the administrative wing where royal feet seldom trod. Nina had been marched here after she'd pleaded her case to a succession of palace guards, starting with the ones at the looming gate. They had finally transferred her into the care of the palace staff and she had been brought here by the sniffiest, most disdainful butler she had ever encountered.

But that was par for the course in the underbelly of a royal household. Nina tried to make herself comfortable on a settee that had likely been built for the express purpose of making interlopers squirm. No wonder it was down here in the basement, the domain of all manner of petty cruelties and intense jockeying for position. Down here—and it was always the same, no matter what kingdom or huffy principality—it was really more the palace of gorgons than gods.

Because the royals were bad enough. Kings and queens with their reigns and their wars and their commandments were all very well, though they did tend to litter princes and princesses about—all primed by lives of excess to behave as atrociously as possible.

They almost couldn't help themselves,

what with all that blue blood making them so constitutionally obnoxious.

It was the people who trailed about after royalty, obsequious and scheming, that Nina truly couldn't stand. The palace courtiers and uppity staff. They *could* have helped themselves but chose not to. However subservient they were when faced with the royalty they served, that was exactly how cutthroat they were behind the scenes. It might as well still be the Dark Ages, when the wrong whisper in the right ear led straight to beheadings.

There might not be too many beheadings with a blade these days, because monarchies were ever more concerned with their images. These days, beheadings were performed in the press, reputations were slashed with a single headline, and on and on the courtiers whispered gleefully, as if actual lives weren't ruined because of their games.

Why swing a blade when you could gossip to the same end?

Nina knew all of this entirely too well, and too personally. She'd been the primary lady-in-waiting to Her Royal Highness, Princess Isabeau of Haught Montagne, a small kingdom high in the Alps, since the day before her sixteenth birthday. A role she had not wanted, had not liked, and should have been overjoyed to lose six months ago.

Alas, her exit had been…complicated.

She was brooding about those complications as she fidgeted in her uncomfortable seat. The palace guards had confiscated her personal effects, so she couldn't distract herself from what she was doing. No mobile. No snacks.

It really was torture.

And then her baby kicked inside her, no doubt as cranky without a snack as Nina was—but the sensation made her smile. She smoothed her hands over her belly, murmuring a little to soothe them both.

Soon enough, someone would come and get her. And then, at some point or another, she would be face-to-face with the creature responsible for the state she was in—a state that required, once again, that she concern herself with the doings of royalty when that was the last thing she wanted.

Some people went their whole lives without encountering a person of royal blood. Nina couldn't seem to stop tripping over them. Though tripping was not how she would describe her last encounter with the arrogantly named Zeus.

Prince Zeus.

Even thinking that name made her...determined.

Nina clung to that word. She was determined, that was all. To see this through. To acquit herself appropriately. To handle this situation as well as possible, for the sake of her child.

To do the right thing—without going down the rabbit hole of blame. She was determined, and that was enough. Because she didn't like any of the other words she could have chosen to describe her current state.

She sighed and returned her attention to this palace and her officious little waiting room. All the furnishings here were too big, too formal, for a palace made all in glorious white—the better to beckon the sea, the guidebooks simpered.

When, once upon a time, the always overconfident Theosian monarchs had been far more concerned with commanding the sea than beckoning it.

The original Theosian castle lay in ruins at the far end of the island that made up the kingdom. Nina had seen it out her window as she'd flown in today from Athens. The parts that were still standing looked suitably cramped and dark, unlike the high ceilings and open archways that made the Palace of the Gods such a pageant of neoclassical eighteenth-century drama.

She'd spent the past few months studying this place as she'd slowly come to terms with what she was going to have to do. And that it was inevitable that she would actually have to come here. Sometimes she'd managed to lose herself a little in the studying, the way she had when she'd first found herself with Isabeau—and would have given anything to escape.

Nina had not had the opportunity to go off to university. Had Isabeau not chosen Nina on her desperate orphanage campaign—the Princess's attempt to show that she was benevolent in the wake of one of her many scandals—Nina would have woken up the next day released from the hold of the state at last. She would have gone out into the world, found her own way, and been marvelously free— but likely would not have studied anything. She'd always tried to remind herself of that.

Isabeau could not have cared less about the private tutoring sessions her father insisted she take. Half the time she hadn't bothered to turn up.

That had left Nina with the very finest tutors in Europe at her disposal. She'd loved every moment of her education, and she'd taken the overarching lesson with her through the years since. If she was to be forced to trail about after Isabeau, she might as well make something of the experience. She'd studied, therefore, every castle, palace, private island, and other such glorious place she found herself, dragged along with Isabeau's catty entourage wherever the Princess went. She'd studied the places and all the contents therein as if she expected she might have to sit an exam on the material.

What Nina really loved was the art all these noble-blooded people tended to hoard. Museums were lovely, but the real collections were in the private homes of collectors with bloodlines—and fortunes—that soared back through the ages. Nina had loved nothing more than sneaking away while Isabeau was entertaining one of her many lovers to take a turn about the gallery of whatever stately place they were trysting in.

That was how she knew that the painting that took up most of the wall opposite her, rather ferociously, was a satirical take on a courtier type some three hundred years ago. And it was comforting, almost, to think that those sorts had always been appalling. It made sense. As long as there were kings, courtiers swarmed.

She was telling her unborn baby about the history of Theosia—ancient Macedonians this, ancient Venetians that—when, finally, the door to her chamber opened.

Nina braced herself, but, of course, it wasn't Prince Zeus who stood there. She doubted the Prince knew this part of the palace existed. Instead, it was the starchy-looking butler who managed to give her the impression that he was curling his thin lip at her without actually moving a single muscle in his face.

It was impressive, Nina thought. Truly.

"Were you speaking with someone?" he asked, each syllable dripping with scorn. He had introduced himself the same way when he'd brought her here. *I am Thaddeus*, he had intoned.

"Yes," Nina said. They stared at each other, and she patted her bump. With, admittedly, some theatrical flair. "The royal child currently occupying my womb, of course."

She might have drawn out the word *womb*.

And it was worth it, because she had the very great pleasure of sitting there, smiling serenely, as the man battled to conceal his distaste. Not because he was trying to spare her feelings, she knew. But because it had no doubt occurred to him that said occupant of her womb might, in fact, turn out to be the heir to the kingdom, and a good servant never burned a bridge if he could help it.

She was all too aware of how these people thought.

After all, she'd been one of them. Not quite staff, not quite a courtier, and therefore condescended to on all sides.

Nina had not missed it.

"If you'll follow me, miss," said the man, all cool disdain and not-quite-repressed horror. Not to mention a subtle emphasis on *miss*, to remind her she had no title or people or, in his view, any reason whatsoever to be here. *I have seen a great many tarts*, his tone assured her, *and vanquished them all*. "His

Royal Highness has deigned to grant you an audience after all."

Nina had been told repeatedly that it would not be possible to see the Prince. If indeed Zeus was even here, which perhaps he was not, none could say—despite the standard that flew today, high above the palace, which was how the Prince informed his people he was in residence. She had only smiled calmly, explained and reexplained the situation, and waited.

And, when necessary, shared both her unmistakable belly as well as photographic evidence of the fact that, yes, she knew the Prince. Yes, in *that* way.

Because while it was probably not helpful to any palace staff to ask them to think back to a scandal six months ago—given how many scandals Prince Zeus was involved in on a daily basis—not all of them had been splashed about in all the international papers. Apparently, she really was special.

Nina ignored the little tug of an emotion she did not care to recognize, smiling the sharp little smile she'd learned in the Haught Montagne court.

"How gracious of the Prince to attend to

his mistakes," she murmured. "How accommodating."

Then she took her time standing up, a basic sort of movement she had never given any thought to before. But it was different at six months pregnant.

Everything was different at six months pregnant.

She found she rather enjoyed seeing the faintest hint of a crack in the butler's facade as he watched her ungainly attempts to rise. More ungainly than necessary, to be sure, but she was the pregnant woman here. They were treating her like she'd done it to herself.

When she most certainly had not—but it would help no one, least of all her child, if she let herself get lost in images that served no one. She already knew how little it served *her*, because she dreamed about that night all the time already, and always woke alone and too hot and riddled with that *longing*—

Stop it, Nina ordered herself crossly.

She kept her expression placid with the aid of years of practice, having had to hide herself in the orphanage and Princess Isabeau's entourage alike. Then she followed the snooty butler out of the antechamber, up from the bowels of the palace, and through the hushed, gleaming halls that were all about airiness and timeless glory, as if gods truly did walk here.

Nina was impressed despite herself.

She kept catching sight of herself in this or that gleaming surface. As ever, she was taken aback by the fact that her belly preceded her. But she was perfectly well acquainted with the rest of the package. *Here comes our Dumpy!* Isabeau would trill, pretending that it was an affectionate nickname. *Hurry, little hen,* she would say as Nina trailed along behind her, forced to keep a smile on her face and her thoughts on such nicknames to herself.

Isabeau had believed that she was being hurtful. And given that being hurtful was one of the main joys in Princess Isabeau's pampered life, it had taken everything Nina had to keep the fact that she was in no way hurt to herself. Snide remarks from a royal princess really didn't hold a candle to daily life in the orphanage, but Isabeau didn't have to know that.

But Isabeau saw her as a hen, so a hen Nina became. She dressed as frumpily as possible, because it annoyed the Princess, herself a fashion icon. Not only were the clothes she chose not quite right, she made sure they never fit her correctly. She made a grand mess of her hair and pretended she didn't understand what was the matter with it.

And she took particular pleasure in forever eating sweets and cakes *at* Isabeau, whose strident dedication to her figure bordered on fanatical.

Nina found she rather liked the hennishness of it all today, though. There were many ways she could have dressed for this encounter, but she'd chosen the maternity outfit that most made her look like the side of a barn. She could have done her hair, or at least brushed it. Instead, she'd opted to let it do as it would, frizzing about of its own accord. Like a rather unkempt blond halo, she thought, pleased, when she saw herself in the polished surface of an ancient mask—hanging there on the wall in bronze disapproval.

Thaddeus was striding forth briskly, clearly trying to hasten their pace, so she slowed her walk to an ungainly waddle. Then only smiled blandly when the man tried to hurry her along. And went even slower.

She was determined to do what was right, or she wouldn't have come here.

But that didn't mean she couldn't enjoy herself in the process.

That had been her philosophy throughout her indentured servitude to the Princess. She was the little orphan girl plucked from obscurity and expected to live in perpetual cringing gratitude for every scrap thrown her way, when she would have been perfectly happy to be left to her own devices in her gutter, thank you. She had perfected the downcast look, with an unreadable curve of her lips that fell somewhere between possible sainthood and the expected servility. Depending on who was looking at her.

But she made her own fun all the same. Her clothes. Her constant sweet and cake consumption, leaving her forever covered in crumbs, which had sent Isabeau into rages. She'd often pretended not to understand the things Isabeau asked of her, forcing her to ask repeatedly. And she had been known to affect deafness when most likely to make the Princess go spare.

A subject of the house of Haught Montagne

could not openly defy her Princess, of course. That was unthinkable.

But there were always ways.

Nina reminded herself that she'd found those ways once and could do it again, as she walked through another set of gilded arches. More gilded than before, in fact. Her hands crept over her belly, where the baby was moving around, making itself known. She had not actually intended for this last, final act of rebellion, she could admit, if only to herself. She'd thought that she was perfectly all right with the consequences as they were.

But that was when the consequences were being ejected from Isabeau's service and called a national disgrace, among a great many other, less polite names, in an endless slew of articles that were always sourced from unnamed people in Isabeau's circle— the curse of the courtiers.

These consequences were a bit different than a bit of scandal and being called mean names by terrible people, she thought, leaving one hand on her belly as she walked.

And that same fierce, mad love blazed through her again, the way it did so often these days. Maybe she hadn't planned this baby, but she wanted it. She had never loved anything the way she loved the tiny human inside her. The little gift she couldn't wait to meet.

She reminded herself that today was all about determination. Nothing more.

Thaddeus flung open a suitably impressive set of doors with all attendant fanfare, then led Nina inside.

"Your Royal Highness," he intoned, "may I present Miss Nina Graine. Your…guest."

Nina blinked as she looked around, and it took her a moment to get her bearings. She found herself in a vast room flooded with light that poured in from exquisitely arched openings on three sides. They were not so much windows as graceful doors that let in all that Mediterranean blue, the boundless sun, and the far-off call of wheeling seabirds. There was the hint of riotous bougainvillea on the terrace outside, and the breeze brought in the scent of honeysuckle and jasmine.

She knew she was standing in a room in the palace—very likely the royal version of a lounge—but it seemed more like some kind of temple.

And as if summoned by that thought alone,

there was suddenly a far brighter gleam where the sun was brightest, until it detached itself from such lesser light and became a man.

Not just any man.

Zeus.

Bathed in light as if he'd conjured it and wearing nothing but a pair of flowing white trousers that clung low on his hips.

Nina hated herself, but that didn't stop the way the sight of him rolled through her, like a song from on high. Except this song came with heat and licked over her. Her breasts. Her belly. The softness between her legs.

Focus, she ordered herself. He was magnificent, but as a person saddled with the name Zeus, he would have to be. He had clearly taken his name as a lifelong challenge.

A challenge he had met, if not exceeded.

And Nina couldn't help but remember, with an unhelpful vividness, that she knew every inch of him.

Zeus moved closer, somehow looking regal and glorious when he was barefoot and wearing the princely version of pajama bottoms. She tried her best to find him ridiculous, with that dark blond hair that looked forever tousled and the half smile that appeared welded to his lips, but she couldn't quite get there. Instead, she was struck by the similarity between him and that bronze mask she'd seen out in the palace halls.

He looked ancient. Almost forbidding, so severely drawn were his features. If she hadn't known better, she would have sworn that he could only have been carved from stone or forged from metal. There was no possibility he could be a man of flesh and blood.

But Nina knew better.

Still he came toward her, until she could see the green of his wicked eyes. And then, sure enough, that slow, edgy curve of his sculpted lips.

She braced herself for that inescapable magnetism of his that she had always thought ought to be bottled, so it could be used as a weapon. It was that fierce. That intense. It seemed to fill the room, closing around her so it was impossible to pretend that she was anything but captivated, no matter how little she wished to be. Her pulse was a racket inside her veins. Her heart thudded.

Even her baby stopped kicking, as if awed.

But far more concerning was the melting

sensation that swept over her, making the fire in her burn hotter. Brighter.

As if she hadn't already gotten into enough trouble with this man.

Prince Zeus of Theosia did not say a word. He put his hands on his lean hips, still with that half smile, as if this was all deeply entertaining, and took a long, slow circle around her. Studying her like she was a cow on a market block in the kind of medieval keeps this man's relatives had ruled over when the earth was young.

When he made it back around to her front, his face was transformed with laughter.

Her heart stopped. Then kicked back into gear, so hard it was painful.

Nina had prepared a brief, informative little speech so she could get the practicalities out of the way and then get back to her life. And she would have told anyone who asked—though no one ever had—that she was not the least bit intimidated by royalty of any stripe. In her case, familiarity really had bred contempt. She wanted no part of hereditary laziness, ceremonial scepters in place of any hint of kindness, or too many thrones instead of thoughtfulness.

And yet she couldn't seem to make her mouth work the way it should.

"I remember you," Zeus said after a long moment of that face of his, far too beautiful for any mortal man.

But he said it as if that surprised him. That it was not that she was in any way memorable, but it was deeply amusing to him that he should recognize her.

As if it was a great compliment to a woman who stood before him, her reason for being here clear enough, as she was swollen with his child.

Nina was sick to death of these royals.

"Are you certain?" she asked crisply, ignoring all that stunning male beauty. Not to mention her memories and the chaos inside. She also ignored the way his brows rose at her tone. "You've had more than a legion or two, I imagine, and there's no telling how many have turned up with claims like mine. Easy to get them all mixed up. You should take a closer look, surely. I could be anyone."

CHAPTER TWO

THE LITTLE BROWN hen clucking at him was…
unexpected.

Yet unexpected was not boring.

And His Royal Highness, Crown Prince
Zeus of Theosia, had been bored beyond all
reason for entirely too long. Since the last
time he'd seen her, not that he cared to think
too closely about his curious reactions to that
night. He'd put them aside and had quickly returned to his usual state of tedium. That was
the trouble with declaring oneself rebellious
at a young age and then pursuing each and
every potential rebellion that arose thereafter
with intensity and commitment.

It turned out that a man could not live on
sin alone.

Zeus had certainly tried.

"A legion or two, perhaps," he agreed,

moving toward the bizarre apparition in the vague shape of a woman who had somehow braved the palace gates and found her way here. A task many had tried, but most had failed. Resoundingly. He received weekly reports on the women who attempted to skirt security and chase him down. That she had succeeded was…not boring at all. "A gentleman does not count such things."

"No need when the tabloids count for you."

He stopped before her, taking in this strange little creature who had scurried around in the wake of Princess Isabeau for all these years. She looked much as she had during the years of his irksome arranged engagement. Dressed to accentuate every possible flaw on her body. Her hair an obvious afterthought. Isabeau had always cultivated glamour, and yet in the background of too many of her photos had lurked her little pet.

Impervious to criticism. Unmoved by commentary.

Zeus had come to see Miss Nina Graine as a kind of symbol. Perhaps, particularly last summer, he had ascribed to her a great many motivations and inner thoughts she did not possess. He had spent more time than he liked to admit conjuring her into an unlikely hero-ine, the better to suit his schemes.

Then he'd discovered the truth. Beneath all the stories he'd told himself and more, be-neath each and every one of the masks she'd ever worn. And the truth had nearly burned him alive.

He didn't like to think about that too much.

Or the fact that her disappearance after their night together had…bothered him.

Zeus allowed himself a smile now as he gazed down at her, returned to all her frumpy splendor. "Most women who claw their way past the palace guard for an audience with me are of a certain stripe. They are not you, however. They do not *actually* convince poor Thaddeus to bring them before me."

Isabeau's hen did not smile. She did not flutter, as women so often did in his pres-ence, like so many small and hapless birds in need of a strong hand to perch upon. She only gripped her enormous, pregnant belly—a development Zeus doubted very much was unrelated to her appearance in his rooms, yet did not wish to consider too closely just yet—and glared at him.

Glared, when he was used to obliging sighs and simpering calf's eyes.

How novel.

"Is that meant to be flattering?" Nina demanded.

When, as a rule, no one dared make demands of him. Unless they were his perpetually unamused father, who never did anything but. And was eternally disappointed at Zeus's refusal to meet them.

His fondest rebellion yet.

"Your memory losses are your own business," Nina was saying in that same distinctly unsimpering manner. "But you must have me confused for one of those women you can't remember if you think I'd find your inability to recall the faces of the women you've slept with to be anything but sad. For you."

Zeus was unrepentant. "I always remember *some* part of the women gracious enough to share themselves with me. It is not always their faces, I grant you. Shall I tell you what I recall of you?"

"I think not. My memory is not clouded with excess. *I* know what happened that night."

She did not exactly *thrust* her belly at him,

but Zeus eyed it like it was a weapon all the same. Still, he wasn't ready to go there. He was intrigued for the first time in as long as he could remember—*six months, perhaps*, a voice in him suggested slyly—and besides, he was perfectly capable of plotting his next move while appearing to be nothing more than the sybaritic fool he'd been playing too well for too long.

He lived in that space. Owned it, even.

Zeus shoved his hands in his trouser pockets and endeavored to look as if, given the faintest push, he might actually lounge about in midair.

"If you mean you did me a great service, I certainly remember that," he said lazily. "Have you gone to all this trouble so that I might thank you? Perhaps an investiture of some kind? I do wish I'd known to dig out the ceremonial swords."

"I shouldn't be at all surprised that you've rewritten what happened to suit yourself." She rolled her eyes—another gesture that Zeus did not usually see before him. Who would dare? No matter how little he seemed to stand upon ceremony, he was still the

Crown Prince of Theosia. "I think we both know that you used me."

"I?" Zeus laughed then. He had wanted something novel, something more than this morbid waiting game he had no choice but to be mired in. He hadn't thought to specify what it was he wanted, and lo, she had appeared. "*I* used *you*? I was under the impression it was the other way around. I have long felt that my primary function is to provide scandals on command, the better for a certain kind of woman to be forced to leave a life she secretly never liked in the first place."

The creature before him scowled, her wild blond hair bobbing slightly from where it was inadequately knotted atop her head. "That is not a *function*. You say it like you've made toying with sad women your own cottage industry."

"I do what I can," Zeus murmured, as if attempting to be humble. A state of being he did not recognize, personally. What purpose could it serve? "No, no, your gratitude alone is my reward."

"Don't be ridiculous," huffed the little brown hen. "I was nothing but a servant.

You, on the other hand, were not only a royal prince, destined for a throne—"

"Not just any throne," he added helpfully. "The humbly named Throne of Ages. It's right down the hall if you want to take a peek. Maybe snap a few pictures? I hear that's all the rage."

"You were also engaged," Nina continued doggedly. "To be married. Since the very day of her birth, if I remember it rightly, as set up by your fathers in an agreement that all of Europe knows inside and out. Given how many times it's been trotted out in the tabloids while one or the other of you was caught entertaining someone outside the bonds of your arrangement."

"Such busybodies, fathers," Zeus murmured. "Don't you think? Forever arranging things on their own and then acting surprised that no one wishes to be an *arrangement*."

"I wouldn't know," she replied coolly. Censoriously, even. "My father died when I was five, and the only arrangements that were ever made for me involved orphanages or princesses."

"Neither of which you liked all that much, if memory serves."

"We have already established that you have pervasive memory issues," she shot back, her chin tilting up. "I will remind you that you were not only the Crown Prince of Theosia that night. You were not only engaged. You were engaged *to my mistress*."

That had rather been the point.

Though, admittedly, Zeus had gotten sidetracked. How could he have known that Isabeau's little hen was hiding the curves of a goddess beneath the outlandish and unflattering things she wore?

And Zeus was, at heart, a connoisseur of the female form.

He had spent six months assuring himself that was all he was, especially when it came to her.

"Darling Isabeau, the most poisonous viper in all of Europe," he said now with a sigh, fairly certain that Nina would not care for any rhapsodizing about her charms. She looked as if she might bite him. "Such a tender union that would have been."

The fact that Isabeau was fake and unpleasant, at best, had not been the reason Zeus hadn't wanted to marry her. Zeus didn't want to marry anyone. He had been making his

sentiments known for years and had questioned the arrangement he'd had no hand in
making—but his royal fiancée had been nothing if not ambitious. Her kingdom was little
more than an uppity ski slope, and that wasn't
enough for Isabeau. She'd had big dreams
of what it would mean to be the Theosian
Queen.

Fidelity hadn't factored in.

Zeus had needed to find a way to make her
break things off before her thirtieth birthday,
as stipulated in the contracts his father had
signed a lifetime ago. It was that or pay outrageous penalties. Like ransoming off one
of the outlying Theosian islands, which even
Zeus, for all his game playing, could not justify. Or countenance.

His ancestors would have risen from the
dead in protest. And really, his father was
quite enough. Zeus couldn't imagine having
more family around to shout at him about
bloodlines and duties and the debt he owed
to history.

The perfect solution had come to him in
a blast of inspiration during a deathly boring dinner engagement on one of his trips to
Haught Montagne—the trips he put off as

long as possible, until Isabeau's father began to make threats of violence. Which in their world could lead to war—whether in the markets or the streets. Neither was acceptable, for obvious reasons.

Or so Zeus had been constantly told by his father for the whole of his life.

Though Zeus had been entertaining himself by imagining otherwise at that dinner. Then he'd spied Isabeau's pet and his plotting had gone off in an entirely different direction. Zeus had been deeply pleased with himself.

But that night had not gone according to plan.

He was blessed with the ability to see the beauty in any woman he encountered. And so he did, and had. Yet what he had not anticipated was that Nina was wholly unlike the other courtiers and ladies who circled his unwanted bride-to-be. Her innocence had awed him. Her enthusiasm had left a permanent mark.

And it turned out a man did not have to look hard for the beauty in Nina. She was hiding it. Deliberately. But he'd found her out.

The truth he did not intend to share was

that he, Zeus of Theosia, had actually thought about her in the months since that night.

More than once.

And at the start, he had done more than *think* about her—

But he barely admitted that to himself.

"You are welcome, Your Royal Highness," Nina was saying in that sharp way he remembered from that evening in Haught Montagne, when he'd found his way beneath all those layers she wore. So deliciously sharp up close when she seemed so soft from a distance. "What a pleasure it was to break off your engagement for you, since you were apparently unable to do it yourself."

But Zeus could not be shamed. Many had attempted it. All had fallen short. He merely lifted a shoulder. "If I had broken it myself, there would have been too many unpleasant consequences. Monies to be paid. Kings to placate. Wars to avert. Far better all round to make Isabeau break it herself." He inclined his head in her direction. "You, apparently, were the bridge too far."

Nina made a noise of frustration. He found it cute.

Yes. *Cute.*

More unforeseen reactions. Zeus hardly knew what to do with himself.

"Your assorted scandals never bothered her." Nina scowled up at him. "Why should they? She always enjoyed her own fun. It was that it was me, her dumpy charity case that she was saddled with because the palace worried she seemed too unlikable. But then, you know this. It's why you chose me."

"Surely lightning struck us both. That is how I recall it."

"It was a clear night in summer." She shook her head. "We were not engaged in the same enterprise, I think."

"Little hen," he chided her. "You break my heart, which is nothing, as anyone will tell you. It is but a cheap little trinket. But you also poke at my pride. A dangerous game. I am not only certain that we were, both of us, very much engaged in the same glorious enterprise that night. But that you enjoyed yourself thoroughly."

Zeus remembered more about that night than he wanted to. He remembered the heat, the unexpected longing, the blast of unconquerable desire. He remembered the way his lips had moved over hers and the responses he had coaxed from her.

How it had all become need and flame—then burned out of control. So bright and greedy that instead of the happy, carefree seduction he'd intended, all charm and release, he'd had no choice but to throw himself into it.

Headfirst.

And he might have spent the past six months telling himself he remembered very little about that night, but that was a lie.

He remembered everything.

Her taste. Her scent.

The small sounds she'd made in the back of her throat.

"I'm afraid the night dims a bit in my memory," she said now, her brown eyes glittering. And she was lying. He could see that she was lying, but in a way, that was more fascinating. "Given what happened the next morning."

She looked at him as if she expected he might collapse in paroxysms of shame at that. Sadly for her, he was still…himself.

"Desperate times," he said, with the grin that had gotten him out of more scrapes than he could count.

And he could see that she was not unaffected. But she did not giggle or melt. She frowned.

"I'm embarrassed to say that it took me some time to work out what had actually happened," she said. Without the faintest hint of a giggle. "Then I realized. You called them. You *personally invited* the paparazzi in that morning."

"I am devastated to discover that you were so misled in your assessment of my character." Zeus enjoyed watching her brow furrow all the more. "Were you truly under the impression that I was or am a good man?"

Though he remembered, little as he might wish to, that making love to this woman had made him wish he was. If only because the gift of her sweet innocence had demanded it.

But it had been too late.

"I have never thought you were anything but you." And that was what made her smile at last, edgy as that smile was. At least it looked like a real one. "If anything, understanding the role you played in this has helped make my course of action clear."

She looked down at the belly between them. He did the same.

But luckily, he'd now had some time to think about the opportunity she presented.

Zeus always had liked an opportunity.

Especially if it helped stick the knife in deeper.

"I do hate to be indelicate," he began. She let out a laugh, and he grinned. "You're quite right. I don't. But you must know that there's almost no purpose to this confrontation scene you have planned, all tears and recriminations followed swiftly by demands—"

"You've had this conversation often, have you?"

He offered her a bland smile. "A great many women assume they must be carrying my child, simply because they wish it to be so."

Her brows lifted. "You being such a paragon of fatherhood and all."

"I'm sure that's the draw." He inclined his head. "Unless and until a DNA test proves that you're carrying my child, this can only be a theoretical conversation. A parade of what-ifs, all destined to end in nothing." Zeus shrugged with a wholly unaffected lack of concern. "I have always enjoyed these things."

She eyed him. "How many children do you have, then?"

"Theoretical children any number of distraught women have claimed must be mine? Pick a number, then multiply it. Real children? Not a one." He allowed himself a smile, perhaps a little more real than necessary. When he usually preferred to hide anything real. There was something about this woman—but he brushed that off. "Perhaps that has something to do with the fact that I do not partake in unprotected sex."

Yet even as he said that, hadn't he gotten a little too enthusiastic with Nina? He remembered that he had been…a little too intense. All of that fire had been such an unexpected wallop. There had been a little too much bathing in it. A little too much wishing that he hadn't already set the wheels in motion that would end their encounter with a shower of flashbulbs.

Something in him seemed to roll over, then hum.

Almost like…anticipation.

He hardly recognized it.

"You may give me any tests you like," she was saying with a dismissive wave of her hand. No tears. No caterwauling. None of the performance of pregnancy that he'd come to expect from this scene. "I've come to inform you of your impending fatherhood, and you may do with that information anything you wish. Summon your doctors and lab technicians at will. Oh, and congratulations."

Zeus wondered if his mask had slipped a little when she paused a moment, that dent between her brows returning. He made sure to look as bored as possible until she cleared her throat and carried on.

"I'll catch you up on what happened after you invited the tabloids in." She paused as if waiting for him to toss in an apology. He didn't, of course. But something in him almost wanted to, and that was unnerving enough. "I was cast out of all royal circles. As this was, in fact, the goal I've been striving toward since Isabeau first took it upon herself to force me under her wing, I was quite pleased. Until…"

She only lifted a hand, indicating her belly. "I thought I was ill. Or perhaps detoxing from too long in Isabeau's presence. Either way, it took me quite some time to understand what had happened to me. And even longer to accept it."

"So long that any other alternatives were no longer available to you," he said, smoothly enough, though he found—to his great surprise—that he had a certain distaste for the notion, as it involved this woman and this baby.

But Nina jerked back as if he'd slapped her.

"I'm an orphan," she said matter-of-factly, though he could see far more emotion in her brown gaze, gone as dark as the bitterest coffee now. His favorite. "This baby is the only family I have."

Something seemed to roar inside him then, shocking Zeus. And he had not been shocked by anything in…six long months. It reminded him a little too closely of that night they'd shared, the shock of all that heat where he'd expected an easy, forgettable pleasure.

Nina had come out of nowhere with a sucker punch yet again.

"I can't say I had any particular intention of sharing this news with you," Nina was saying. "I thought that perhaps I could simply live my life, as I always wanted, with no royal nonsense to consider." She shrugged. "I'm afraid I know too much."

"About royalty?" He nodded sagely. "A tragedy indeed."

"One does not require a great deal of knowledge about royalty," she shot back at him. "They rule things. The end. Everything you need to know about your average, run-of-the-mill member of any royal family can be summed up like so. It's what makes them so presumptuous."

Zeus could not deny that. What astounded him was that…he wanted to.

But Nina was still speaking. "No, what I know too much about is the tabloids. The paparazzi. Just because I've enjoyed six months to myself doesn't mean my solitude will continue. Sooner or later, someone will remember me. Then they'll all find me. And worse, my baby."

She rubbed that belly of hers again, currently housed in a dress he suspected might possibly have been used as a circus tent. When he knew that her actual figure was so sweet and ripe that he found himself hungry even now. For he could see—what little of her he could truly see—that this pregnancy had ripened her further.

Zeus had the blistering notion that he actually *wanted* her to be carrying his child. He *wanted* this ripeness to be his. All his.

He shoved that aside.

Because he couldn't believe such a notion could cross his mind, much less bloom the way it seemed to be doing.

"Are you saying that the paparazzi have already found you?" he managed to ask past what amounted to a full-scale riot inside of him.

A riot her ripeness, so close to him, did not help.

"I don't think they have, but who can say where a photographer with a nasty telephoto lens might lurk?" Again, that edgy smile. "The more my pregnancy shows, the more likely someone is to do the math. It will be worse once the baby comes."

"I see. You thought you'd come to me and try to get ahead of mathematics."

"No, it occurred to me that the math being what it is, I can expect that whether I wanted to involve you or not, you would end up involved." She sniffed. "Now or later. I decided to come ahead of the inevitable exposé to let you know what my demands are."

"See? I told you there would be demands." He smiled benevolently at her and found it delightful when she gritted her teeth in response. Far easier to deal with that sort of thing than any *ripening*. Much less his response to it. He was going to have to sort himself out. Later. "There are always demands. It's almost as if demands are the point of these little scenes."

"I've researched Theosian law," she said, without any indication she'd heard his comments. And Zeus was not used to being so soundly and repeatedly ignored. He couldn't tell if he hated it…or if his reaction was a bit more intense. And was something more like admiration. "Apparently, one of your ancestors so enjoyed spreading himself about that it was written into law that all royal bastards must be given a certain stipend from the crown. To keep them in an appropriate style, though not under the same roof, as that might offend any given queen."

Zeus laughed out loud. Of all the things he'd imagined she might say, it wasn't that.

"Ah, yes, the bastard clause." The clause

that every young royal Theosian man was lectured about extensively as he set to head out into the world and misbehave. He hadn't heard it mentioned by anyone outside the palace staff in ages—no doubt because he was considered such a lost cause. "It may surprise you to learn that the clause originated from the betrayed Queen in question, because she preferred to make public her husband's indiscretions. I think you'll find we haven't used it here in generations."

"Then I suppose I've come to ask for the usual amount of support," Nina replied easily enough, though her chin notched higher. "I'm not one for charity. I've already spent a lifetime being force-fed it while being told how grateful I should be for each and every sour bite. If it were up to me, you would never have seen me again. I would have made my own way in this world, and happily. That was my intention."

"So you have now stated twice." Zeus sighed. "I do hope you're not going to get boring on me. That would be a tragedy indeed."

She did not look like she agreed. And the Theosian sun made love to her as she stood there, facing off with him. It danced over the spun straw of her hair and the sensual bow of her lips. It was the sort of light that most women of his acquaintance avoided, and for good reason.

But it only made Nina that much more beautiful.

Inarguably lovely.

You need to remember who you are, a stern voice within him piped up then.

"I found a perfectly decent situation in England," she told him. "It would be hard, of course, but I'm not afraid of hard. I believed I could do it. I began to think I *would* do it, damn it…" Nina smiled a little ruefully. "Until it occurred to me that this baby is neither an orphan nor a prince. He or she should not have to pay for the sins of either."

Zeus heard a swift intake of breath. It took him a moment to realize it was his.

Nina straightened her shoulders. "Just as this baby doesn't deserve the lengths I'm willing to go to for freedom, it also doesn't deserve to be cut off from the kind of life it could have, just because its father is you."

An uncomfortable sensation worked its way through Zeus then, though it took him far too long to recognize it. Much less name it.

But he was fairly certain it was temper. When he had learned, so very long ago, that his own temper was useless and it was far better to poke and prod and play games, so that others could experience theirs and lose control.

He'd learned how to be very, very good at that.

And he had come to think of temper as weakness. Because what was it but emotion, twisted around and easily manipulated by men like him? He allowed himself none of that, either. Yet there was no mistaking it. The curl of a kind of smoke winding around inside him was very clearly temper.

How…astonishing.

"So, like every other woman who has ever pursued me," he said, drawling out the words and making sure no hint of temper leaked through, because he didn't know why it should. He refused to feel such things. Or any things. "You are after me for my money."

And he watched, too fascinated for his own good, as Nina's pretty brown eyes flashed. This orphan, this little brown hen, had never been what she seemed. He did not know how he had suffered through any number of interactions with Isabeau before he'd come to understand that.

But once he'd begun to see her, all too plainly, he couldn't unsee her.

He only saw *more* of her.

She had pride, this creature. And if he wasn't mistaken, a healthy dose of a burning need for retribution about her.

In other words, she was perfect.

"Yes," she said, as if she knew the direction his thoughts had gone. "I want your money. I see no reason this baby shouldn't be raised like the child of a prince it is."

"Then I have some deliciously good news for you," Zeus informed her with a little bow, because he couldn't resist a flourish. Not when his endgame had just altered completely. "Assuming this isn't all an elaborate ruse that will be uncovered shortly by the palace's medical staff, allow me to be the first to congratulate you."

"Why?" she asked, suspicion stamped all over her. "For what?"

Zeus only gazed down at her, that temper still curling around and around inside him, though he was happy to discover it did not inhibit his enjoyment. That would have been a tragedy.

"On your nuptials," he told her.

"My…what?"

"Oh, happy day," Zeus said, letting his voice carry and rebound back from the pristine walls like so much dizzy heat. "We are to be married, little hen. You lucky thing. Women have been jostling for that position since before I was born."

"Not me!" She looked almost insultingly horrified. "I don't want to marry *you*!"

Which, he could admit, was another reason she was perfect. Zeus could not have tolerated any of the women who did actually want to marry him, and quite desperately. They longed for either the man they thought he was or the throne he would take, and either way, it wasn't him.

Only this woman, only Nina, would do.

"I am afraid that what you want does not signify," he said, only the pulse he could feel hammering away in his neck indicating that he was perhaps not as calm as he was pretending. "You should have done more research. If you had, you might have found that here on Theosian soil, the heir to the kingdom belongs to the crown."

Her eyes widened. Almost comically. "That can't possibly mean what I think it does."

Zeus rocked back on his heels, all the strange emotions and memories of this encounter washing over him. But he concentrated on her dismay instead.

"I am the Crown Prince. If you are carrying my heir, I have every right to do with you what I will." He allowed himself a smile then, one that in no way hid the truth of him, and enjoyed it when her eyes widened farther still. "Welcome to Theosia. I hope you like our little island. You will one day reign as Queen."

Nina cemented her place here by looking ill at the very idea. Not triumphant. Not thrilled. *Ill.* "That will never, ever happen. Never."

"Oh, but it will, my little hen," Zeus replied, something perilously close to happy, for once. He told himself it was because the pieces of this last part of his plan were coming together so beautifully. And for no other reason. Because there could not possibly be another reason. Zeus would not allow there to be. "You can depend on it."

CHAPTER THREE

EVERYTHING HAPPENED A little too quickly then.

So quickly that Nina found herself perilously close to dizzy.

Zeus moved across the vast room, striding like a man with purpose instead of the monument to idleness he usually appeared to be in all things. He swung open the doors to his chamber, said two words, and half the palace staff seemed to flow in. He barked out orders, and for all that he lounged about Europe—acting as if he was too lazy to lift his finger when he could find any number of willing women to lift it for him—it was clear that his staff knew this version of him well. Peremptory in the extreme.

Princely, something in her whispered. *A man who is not only used to command, but infinitely comfortable in it.*

That made her head spin enough, because that wasn't Zeus. Not the Zeus the world knew entirely too well.

But the voice within her wasn't done.

Just like that night, it murmured, so that more of that wild heat charged through her, setting her aflame.

The way it had when she'd seen him again. And when he'd called her *little hen*.

Because the Zeus he'd become that night had been...intense. Demanding.

Different.

But she didn't have any time to take any of that in as she was marched from his rooms by a phalanx of aides. Who, at least, acted more polite and solicitous than the initial butler and the whole of the palace guard had. They swept her through the halls of the palace, climbing from one fairy-tale level to the next, one of them talking in a low voice into her mobile as they moved.

They arrived at their destination, another suite of graceful, expertly appointed rooms that looked, on the one hand, like every suite of rooms she had ever stayed in at places like this—though she'd never stayed in one quite as lovely. For this was the Palace of the Gods, so everything was that much brighter and inlaid with gold and silver. As if the light filling every room was not the weather, but a part of the planned decor. She was taken to a small salon, dappled with light that poured in from a shaded balcony outside.

"You will wait here," said the aide with the phone, who Nina suspected was the one in charge. Though the older woman managed to make the very clear command sound as if, maybe, it had been Nina's idea and she was only confirming it.

"I would love to wait," Nina replied as she lowered herself down to a settee that was so much more comfortable than the one she'd been sitting on before that she rather thought they shouldn't share the same name. She sat and smiled up at the woman. "But I'm afraid the baby won't. If I don't eat soon, neither one of us is going to be very happy."

The older woman looked at her moment, then snapped her fingers. Confirming that she was, indeed, in charge of this particular set of staff—and also setting one of her underlings running from the room.

"Then, of course, you shall eat," she said. Nina was almost too grateful to bear it. "If you know where my personal belongings are, I can feed myself. I have snacks in my bag."

"Your personal belongings are being looked over by the palace guard," her aide said, sounding sorrowful. Though her eyes remained shrewd. "Security will do as they like, you know. But not to worry, we'll have something from the kitchens shortly."

And Nina could not have been more surprised when, not five minutes later, the underling reappeared. He was trailed by another staff member pushing a cart, who then began to lay out the makings of a hearty afternoon tea. But in Theosian style, with dishes of grilled fish to go along with finger sandwiches, mountains of vegetables and fresh fruits, hard cheeses, pots of herbed butter, and loaves of fragrant baked bread.

By the time another set of people appeared before her, she felt better than she had all day.

Which was maybe why, when one of the new people introduced herself as a doctor and announced that she was there to check on Nina's health—and the paternity of the baby she carried while they were at it—she was less outraged than she might otherwise have been. Because, as ever, she was a realist. She had known before she came here, no matter how grudgingly, that there was no possibility anyone would simply take her word for it. That was not how powerful men operated, whether they had their own palaces or not.

She followed the doctor and her cheerful, efficient team into the next room, a small study with stacks of books on whitewashed shelves and bright blue flowers in handcrafted vases. And there submitted to all necessary tests. Whatever it took to make her case in a place where her word wouldn't do.

The story of her life, really.

"You must be tired," said the aide from before, coming in to collect her once her exam was done. "After all the traveling, and then such a long day in the palace. Perhaps it would be best if you rested, no? Do feel free to ring should you require anything. Shall we say, a light supper later this evening? The kitchen will bring it up at the hour of your choice."

"I appreciate the concern for my feelings," Nina said dryly. "But I'm not the least bit tired."

"I feel certain you must be," replied the other woman, implacably.

"You could simply say that I'm to be locked in these quarters until such time as the paternity of my baby can be determined," Nina said. Then smiled. "I think we'd both respect each other more, don't you?"

The other woman inclined her head, but her shrewd gaze warmed. "Indeed, miss."

"You may call me Nina." And Nina had the strangest sense of vertigo, because she couldn't recall the last time she'd been the one to offer her first name. She had always been the one who had to mind her manners constantly around her betters.

"I am Daphne," the woman replied. Her mouth curved. "And I will let you know when you're free to move about the palace."

"See?" Nina asked. "Isn't that better?"

Daphne smiled wider, then clapped her hands and emptied the suite, leaving Nina alone.

For a while, she stayed where she was, staring at pretty blue flowers in small earthenware vases while inside of her everything was… Zeus.

That night six months ago was all tangled up in today, a temple of light and all his dark-honeyed glory, as if baklava had taken human form and called itself a prince.

Nina let out a long, shuddery breath.

She got up, then went out of the study into the atrium that took the place of any central hall. She could see into the first salon and was pleased to find they'd left her the remains of her tea, which made her smile despite herself. Because if she needed to, she would have thrown open these doors and stormed the palace kitchens if she was hungry.

Clearly, Daphne knew that and had removed the temptation to leave here.

She walked into the center of the atrium, where a fountain gurgled sedately, appreciating the glass ceiling and the greenery everywhere. Slowly, she turned in a circle. She could see the bedroom beyond two blue doors, a massive four-poster bed set against a wall done in mosaic. There were several other rooms, but their doors were shut, so she could only guess what was behind them. Some of these palatial guest quarters had screening rooms and bowling alleys, their own elevators and private pools. Boardrooms and full offices for government and business-minded guests. Palaces these days were equipped to cater to the needs of visiting royalty and all of their expectations on the high end, and questionable guests like Nina in more self-contained units like this.

And then she laughed at herself, because the atrium alone was larger than any place she'd lived in the last six months. Maybe she'd have been happier if she didn't know it was the sort of smallish suite Princess Isabeau would have sneered at—but deemed good enough for Nina.

She shook off memories of the wretched Isabeau and followed the light. Through the bedroom and out onto the wide balcony that she found waiting for her, wrapping around the side of the corner suite she occupied.

There was a shaded part of the balcony and then a far sunnier bit. Nina went out and stood in the sun for as long as she could, letting the heat sink into her bones and chase away the lingering cold after her last couple of months in England, then she made her way back into the shade. She found the chaise with the best view, straight out into the sea, and settled herself there.

And then, listening to the waves and staring at all that deep blue, she found herself getting drowsy. Despite her claims. She told herself it was all the food she'd just eaten. It had nothing to do with the day she'd had here.

Nina wasn't getting *soft*.

And as she drifted off into sleep, all she could see was that bright, impossible light growing even brighter, and then Zeus stepping out of it, shining far hotter than the lot.

So it wasn't as much of a shock as it might otherwise have been when she woke to find Zeus standing over her once again.

She was glad she'd worn her most hideous skirt, wide like a tent. Because it functioned like bedding, and she knew without having to look that she was properly covered. And then laughed at herself. The man had already seen her naked. That was why she was here in the first place.

Nina rubbed her hands over her eyes, then over the rest of her face, mostly to check to see if she had been caught drooling.

Then she tried to focus on Zeus, standing so still in the kind of dark bespoke suit that she associated with his inevitable presence across all the capitals of Europe. Cut to make him seem even taller, even broader, even more perfectly shaped. A love letter to his perfect body. The sky behind him was turning a deep blue, smudged with orange and pink, from a sun just set, as if it had prettied itself just for him.

And Nina felt breathless, as if the whole world was holding its breath when really, that was just her. She tried to force herself to breathe normally again. She assured herself it had nothing at all to do with the man standing at the foot of her chaise. She was pregnant. Surely she could blame any odd physical sensations on that.

Not on Zeus and the sunset all around him that made him look even more ancient and unworldly.

"I take it you've learned that you're the father of my baby," Nina said.

She blamed the rasp in her voice on her nap.

Zeus only looked at her a long while. The sky continued to put on a show behind him. "It seems we are to be parents, little hen."

And Nina had never minded that nickname from Isabeau. She hadn't liked it, but it hadn't *bothered* her. Isabeau had imagined it held more weight than it did.

year-old any more—nor was she the li[t]
without a mother's love. She was a mother herself now, with her own thriving online business
doing pet portraits—and she'd had her heart broken once before by Ross. In short, she was all
grown up now. She'd worked hard to build a life
for her and her son, and there was no way she'd
throw it all away for some cheap thrills. However tempting.

'Fine, I'm sorry.' The muscle in Conall's jaw
softened and he had the decency to look contrite.
'I overstepped with that remark,' he murmured.
'It's just…' He drew close and gathered her into
a hug. 'I'm your big brother. And I don't want
to see you hurt by him again.'

She softened against him, the comforting
scent of his cologne and the peaty smell of good
Irish single malt whiskey gathering in her throat.
Banding her arms around his waist, she hugged
him back, aware of how far they'd come since
that miserable Christmas morning when Con
had found their mother dead…

She'd pushed her brother away so many
times in the years after that dreadful event,
especially as a teenager, when she'd acted out
at every opportunity—to test his commitment,
she realised now. They'd had some epic shouting matches as a result, but he'd always stuck
regardless. Because Con wasn't just pig-headed
and arrogant with a fiery temper that matched

her own, he was also loyal to a fault and more resilient and hard-wearing than the limestone of the cliffs outside.

Her eyes stung as she drew back to gaze up at his familiar face. 'You've been much more than just a big brother to me, Con. So much more. And I appreciate it. But you've got to trust me on this. I know what I'm doing, okay?'

He drew in a careful breath and let it out slowly, clearly waging a battle with himself not to say any more on the subject. But at last he nodded. 'Okay, Smelly,' he said, using the nickname he'd first coined when—according to family legend—he'd had to change one of her nappies.

She laughed, because he knew how much she'd always hated that fecking nickname. Trust Con to get the final word.

But then he cupped her shoulders and gave her a paternal kiss on the forehead. 'I do trust you,' he murmured. 'And anyhow, if he hurts you again, I'll murder him. So there's that,' he added, only half joking, she suspected.

She forced her lips to lift in what she hoped was a confident smile as her eyes misted.

Now all she needed to do was learn how to trust herself with Ross De Courtney.

Grand! No pressure, then.

CHAPTER FIVE

ROSS STOOD ON the grass near the Kildaragh heliport, next to the company Puma he'd piloted from the airport in Knock to get to Conall O'Riordan's estate without delay what felt like several lifetimes ago, and braced as the O'Riordans headed towards him, en masse.

Carmel had changed out of the silky bridesmaid's dress into a pair of skinny jeans and a sweater, which did nothing to hide the lush contours of her lean body.

He stiffened against the inevitable surge of lust and shifted his gaze to the child—whose hand was firmly clasped in hers. The boy was literally bouncing along beside her, apparently carrying on a never-ending conversation that was making his mother smile.

The pregnant lady and the man he had spotted earlier in the gardens—who Ross had been informed by Katie were the other O'Riordan sibling, Imelda, and her husband, Donal—followed behind them. Conall O'Riordan, Ross's sister, and two footmen carrying a suitcase and assorted other luggage, brought up the rear.

He nodded to Katie as the party approached. He'd spoken to his sister ten minutes ago—a stilted, uncomfortable conversation, in which he'd apologised for disturbing her wedding and she'd apologised for not telling him sooner about his son's existence.

His sister sent him a tentative smile back now, but as Carmel approached him with the boy Katie held back with her husband and in-laws, making it clear they were a united front. United behind Carmel, and Ross was the out-sider.

His ribs squeezed at the stark statement of his sister's defection. Even though he knew it was his own fault. He'd never been much of a brother to her, to be fair. He should have re-paired the rift between them years ago. But thoughts of his sister disappeared, the pang in his chest sharpening, as Carmel reached him with the child.

'Hi, Ross. This is Cormac,' she said. She drew in a ragged breath. 'My son,' she added, her voice breaking slightly. 'He wanted to say hello to you before we left.'

'Hiya,' the little boy piped up, then waved. The sunny smile seemed to consume his whole face, his head tipped way back so he could see Ross properly.

Ross blinked, momentarily tongue-tied, as it occurred to him he had no idea how to even greet the boy.

Going with instinct, because the boy's neck position looked uncomfortable, he sank onto one knee, to bring his gaze level with the child's. 'Hello,' he said, then had to clear his throat when the word came out on a low growl.

But the boy's smile didn't falter as he raised one chubby finger to point past Ross's shoulder to the helicopter. 'Does the 'copter belong to yous?' he asked, the Irish accent only making him more beguiling.

Ross glanced behind him to buy himself some time and consider how to respond, surprised by the realisation that, even though this would most likely be the only time he would ever talk to his son, he wanted to leave a good impression... Or at least not a bad one. 'Yes, it belongs to my company,' he said, deciding to stick with the facts.

'It's bigger than my uncle Con's 'copter,' the little boy shot back.

Ross's lips quirked. 'Is it, now?' he replied, stupidly pleased with the comment.

At least I've managed to best Conall O'Riordan with the size of my helicopter.

The little boy nodded, then tipped his head to one side. 'Does it hurt?' he asked, his fingertip brushing across the swollen area on Ross's jaw.

Ross's throat thickened, the soft, fleeting touch significant in a way he did not understand. 'A bit.'

'It looks hurty,' the boy said. 'Mammy says it's naughty to hit people. Why did Uncle Con hit you?'

'Um, well…' He paused, completely lost for words. The tips of his ears burned as a wave of shame washed through him at the thought of how he and O'Riordan had behaved in front of this impressionable child. What an arse he'd been to take a swing at the man. 'Possibly he hit me because I tried to hit him first,' he offered, knowing the explanation was inadequate at best. 'And missed.'

'Cormac, remember Uncle Con told you it was a mistake and he's sorry.' Carmel knelt next to the boy. 'And I'm sure Ross is sorry too,' she added, sending him a pointed look.

Ross remembered how she'd mentioned she always addressed her son by his full name when he was being disciplined. But the child seemed unafraid at the firm tone she used, his expression merely curious as he wrapped an arm around his mother's neck and leaned into her body.

'I am sorry,' Ross said, because her stern look seemed to require that he answer.

'Yes, Mammy, but…' the little boy began,

turning to his mother and tugging on her hair. 'Still it *was* naughty now…'

'Mr De Courtney, we'll need to leave soon if we're going to make our departure time from Knock,' his co-pilot interrupted them.

'Okay, Brian, thanks.' Ross rose back to his feet. 'If you wish to say your goodbyes, I'll wait in the cockpit,' he said to Carmel, suddenly eager to get away from the emotion pushing against his chest—and the child who could never be a part of his life.

'Okay, I'll only be a minute,' Carmel said, the sheen of emotion in her eyes only making the pressure on his ribcage worse.

He dismissed it. What good did it do? Being intrigued by the boy? Moved, even? When he wasn't capable of forming a relationship with him?

'Goodbye, Cormac,' he murmured to the child, ignoring the fierce pang stabbing under his breastbone.

'Goodbye, Mr Ross,' the boy replied, with remarkable gravity for a child of such tender years. But as Carmel took her son's hand, to direct him back towards her family and say her goodbyes, the little boy swung round and shouted. 'Next time yous come we can play tag. Like I do with Uncle Donal.'

'Of course,' he said, oddly torn at the thought

he'd just made a promise he would be unable to keep… Because there would never be a next time.

'I think, in the circumstances, it would be best if we call a halt to this trip. I can have the helicopter take you back to Kildaragh.'

Carmel swung round to find Ross standing behind her in the private jet they'd just boarded at Knock airport. He looked tall and indomitable, and tired, she thought as she studied him. She waited for her heartbeat to stop fluttering— the way it had been for the last thirty minutes, ever since she had watched him speak to their son for the first time. She needed to get that reaction under control before they got to New York.

'Why would it be best?' she asked.

They'd travelled in silence after she'd bid goodbye to Mac and her family, the noise of the propellors too loud to talk as Ross had piloted the helicopter down the coast to Knock airport. She'd been grateful for the chance to collect her thoughts, still reeling from the double whammy of seeing Ross talk to Mac—and saying goodbye to her baby boy for seven whole nights.

She knew something about luxury travel— after all, her brother was a billionaire—but even so she'd been impressed by how quickly they'd been ushered aboard De Courtney's private jet, which had been waiting on the tarmac when they arrived. But she'd sensed Ross's growing reluctance as soon as they'd boarded the plane, the tension between them only increasing. The smell of new leather filled her senses now as she waited for Ross to reply.

His brow furrowed. 'Surely it's blatantly obvious after my brief conversation with the boy— this trip is pointless?'

'I disagree,' she said, surprised that had been his take away from the encounter.

Certainly, he'd been awkward and ill at ease meeting his son. That was to be expected, as she would hazard a guess he had very little experience of children. But she had also noticed how moved he'd been, even if he didn't want to admit it. And how careful.

'Mac likes you already,' she said, simply.

His frown deepened. 'Then he's not a very good judge of character.'

'On the contrary,' she said, 'he's actually pretty astute for a three-year-old.'

He shoved his hands into the pockets. 'So you still wish to accompany me?' he asked again.

'Yes, I do. If the offer is still open,' she said, suddenly knowing the conversation they were having wasn't just about their son. Because the air felt charged. On one level, that scared her. But on another, after seeing him make an effort to talk to his son openly and honestly, it didn't.

Perhaps he was right. Perhaps this trip was

a lost cause. After all, a week was hardly long enough to get to know anyone. Especially someone who seemed so guarded. But she was still convinced she had to try... And she was also coming to realise that there was more at stake here than just her son's welfare.

Didn't she deserve to finally know what had made her act so rashly all those years ago? She'd thrown herself at this man that night, revelled in the connection they'd shared, and a part of her had always blamed herself for that. Maybe if she got to the bottom of why he had captivated her so, she might be able to forgive that impulsive teenager for her mistakes. And finally let go of the little girl she'd been too, who had looked for love in places where it would never exist.

She waited for him to reply, her breath backing up in her lungs at the thought she might have pushed too hard. It was one of her favourite flaws, after all. And knowing she would be gutted if he backed out now and told her the trip was off.

The moment seemed to last for ever, the awareness beginning to ripple and burn over her skin as he studied her.

His eyes darkened and narrowed. Could he see how he affected her? Why did that only make the kinetic energy more volatile?

'The offer is still open,' he said, at last, and her breath released, making her feel light-headed. But then he stepped closer and touched his thumb to her cheek. He slid it down, making the heat race south, then cupped her chin and raised her face. 'But I should warn you, Carmel. I still want you,' he said, his voice rough with arousal. 'And that could complicate things considerably.'

Her lips opened, her breath guttering out, the anticipation almost as painful as the need as her gaze locked on his and what she saw in it both terrified and excited her. It was the same way he had looked at her all those years ago—focussed, intense—as if she were the only woman in the whole universe and he the only man.

She licked arid lips, and the heat in his gaze flared.

'Do you understand?' he demanded.

She nodded. 'Yes, I feel it too,' she said, not ashamed to admit it. Why should she be? She wasn't a girl any more. 'It doesn't mean we need act on it.'

He gave a strained laugh—then dropped his hand. 'Perhaps.'

'Mr De Courtney, the plane is ready to depart in ten minutes if you and Ms O'Riordan would like to strap yourselves in,' the flight attendant said, having entered the compartment unnoticed by either of them.

Ross's gaze lifted from her face. 'Thank you, Graham. I'm going to crash in the back bedroom. Make sure Ms O'Riordan has everything she needs for the duration of the flight.'

The attendant nodded. 'Of course, sir.'

Without another word to her, Ross headed towards the back of the plane.

She gaped. Had she just been dismissed?

The attendant approached her. 'Would you like to strap yourself in here and then I can show you to the guest bedroom when we reach altitude?'

'Sure, but just a minute…' she said, then shot after her host.

She opened the door she had seen Ross go into moments before. And stopped dead on the threshold.

He turned sharply at her entry, holding his torn shirt in his hand.

Oh. My.

She devoured the sight of his naked chest, her gaze riveted to the masculine display as the heat blazed up from her core and exploded in her cheeks.

The bulge of his biceps, the ridged six-pack defined by the sprinkle of hair that arrowed down beneath the waistband of his trousers, the flex of his shoulder muscles—were all quite simply magnificent.

'Was there something you wanted?' he prompted.

'I… Yes.' She dragged her gaze to his face,

the wry twist of his lips not helping with her breathing difficulties, or her burning face. She sucked in a lung full of air and forced herself to ask the question that had been bothering her for nearly an hour. 'I just wanted to ask you, what made you kneel when you met him? Mac, that is?' she managed, realising the sight of his chest had almost made her forget her own son's name.

He threw away his shirt, clearly unbothered by his nakedness. 'Why do you want to know that?'

'It's just… You say you don't know anything about children. But it was thoughtful and intuitive to talk to him eye to eye like that. I was impressed. And so was Mac.'

'Hmm,' he said, clearly not particularly pleased by the observation. 'And you think this makes me a natural with children, do you?' he said, the bitter cynicism in the tone making it clear he disagreed.

'I just wondered why you did it,' she said, letting her own impatience show. The jury was still out on his potential as a father, and she only had a week to decide if she wanted to let him get to know her son. But she didn't see how they could make any progress on that unless he was willing to answer a simple question. 'That's all.'

'I'm afraid the answer is rather basic and not quite as intuitive as you believe,' he said, still prevaricating.

'Okay?' she prompted.

He sighed. 'My father was a tall man. His height used to intimidate me at that age. I didn't wish to terrify the boy, the way my father terrified me. Satisfied?'

'Yes,' she said, the wave of sympathy almost as strong as the spurt of hope.

Perhaps this didn't have to be a lost cause at all.

He began to unbuckle his belt, his gaze darkening. 'Now I suggest you leave, unless you want to join me in this bed for the duration of the flight.'

'Right.' She scrambled out of the room, slamming the door behind her.

It was only once she had snapped her seat belt into place that it occurred to her she was more excited by his threat than intimidated by it.

Uh-oh.

CHAPTER SIX

WHAT AM I even doing here?

Carmel stood at the floor-to-ceiling window of Ross De Courtney's luxury condo and stared through the glass panes of the former garment factory at the street life below as Tribeca woke up for another day.

The guest room she'd been given was a work of art—all dramatic bare brick walls and vaulted arches, steel columns, polished walnut wood flooring and minimalist furniture, which included a bed big enough for about six people, and an en suite bathroom designed in stone and glass brick. The room even had its own roof terrace, beautifully appointed with trailing vines, wrought-iron furniture and bespoke lighting to create an intimate and yet generous outdoor space.

The views were spectacular, too. At seven stories up she could see the tourist boats on the Hudson River a block away and the New Jersey waterfront beyond, to her left was the dramatic spear of the One World Trade Center building, and below her was the bustle and energy of everyday New Yorkers—dressed in their trademark uniform of business attire and trainers—flowing out of and into the subway station on the corner or dodging the bike couriers and honking traffic to get to work, most of them sporting go-cups of barista coffee.

She knew something about luxury living from the glimpses she'd had of her brother's lifestyle. But Ross De Courtney's loft space, situated in the heart of one of Manhattan's coolest neighbourhoods, was something else—everything she had thought high-end New York living would be and more. But the edgy energy and purpose of all the people below hustling to get somewhere—and the stark modernity of the exclusive space she was staying in—only made her feel more out of place. And alone.

She'd been here for over twenty-four hours already, after arriving on the flight across the Atlantic. And while she'd spent a productive day yesterday—in between several power naps—exploring Ross's enormous loft apartment, the local area, and setting up a workstation with the art supplies she'd brought with her in the apartment's atrium, she'd barely seen anything of the man she'd come here to get to know.

She sighed, and took a sip of the coffee she'd spent twenty minutes figuring out how to brew on his state-of-the-art espresso machine after waking up before dawn.

Thank you, epic jet lag!

He'd dropped her off late at night after their flight and a limo ride from the airport, during which he'd spent the whole time on his phone. Once they'd arrived at the apartment, he'd told her to make herself at home, given her a set of keys and a contact number for his executive assistant, and then headed straight into his offices because he apparently had 'important business'.

And she hadn't seen him since.

She didn't even know if he was in residence this morning. She'd tried to stay up the previous evening, to catch him when he returned from work, but had eventually crashed out at around eight p.m., New York time. And slept like the dead until four this morning. She hadn't heard him come in the night before, and there had been no sign he'd even been in the kitchen last night during her adventures with the espresso machine this morning.

Is he avoiding me?

She took another gulp of the coffee, the pulse of confusion and loneliness only exacerbated by the memory of her truncated conversation over her video messaging app with her baby boy five minutes before.

'Mammy, I can't talk to yous. Uncle Donal is taking me to see the horses.'

'Okay, fella, shall I call you tomorrow?'

'Yes, bye.'

And then he'd been gone, and Imelda had appeared, flushed and smiling. 'Thanks so much for letting us have him for the week, Mel,' she'd said as she cradled her bump. 'We need the practice for when this little one arrives and he's doing great so far. He went to bed without complaint last night.'

'Ah, that's grand, Immy,' she'd replied, stupidly tearful at the thought her little boy was doing so well. Even better than she had expected. And a whole lot better than her.

She missed him, so much.

Not seeing his face first thing when she woke up had been super weird. Especially now she was questioning why she'd flown all this way to get to know a man who didn't seem to want to know her. Or Mac.

'You must contact me if there's any problem at all,' she'd told her sister, almost hoping Imelda would give her the excuse she needed to abandon what already seemed to be a fool's quest. 'I can hop straight on a flight if need be.'

'Sure, of course, but Mac's grand at the moment, he hasn't mentioned missing you once,' Imelda had said, with typical bluntness. Then she had sent Carmel a cheeky grin. 'How's things going with Mac's uber-hot daddy?'

'I'm not here to notice how hot he is, Immy,'

she'd replied sternly, aware of the flush hitting her own cheeks—at the recollection of Ross without his shirt on in the close confines of the jet's bedroom. 'I'm here to get to know him a bit better and discuss Mac with him, and his place in his son's life. That's all.'

'Of course you are, and that's important for sure,' her sister had said, not making much of an effort to keep the mischievous twinkle out of her eyes—which was even visible from three thousand miles away. 'But sure there's no reason now not to notice what a ride he is at the same time.'

Oh, yes, there is, Immy. Oh, yes, there is.

She pressed her hand to her stomach, recalling the spike of heat and adrenaline at her sister's teasing before she'd ended the call, which was still buzzing uncomfortably in her abdomen now. Trust Imelda to make it worse.

The loud ring of the apartment's doorbell jerked her out of her thoughts. And had hot coffee spilling over her fingers. She cursed, then listened intently as she cleaned up the mess and tiptoed to the door of her bedroom to peek out.

If Ross answered the door, she'd at least know if he was here. Then she could waylay him before he left again. Perhaps they could have breakfast together? Although the thought of Ross De Courtney in any kind of domestic setting only unsettled her more.

The bell rang a second time and then she heard something else... Was that a dog barking?

Surprise rushed through her, which turned to visceral heat as the man himself appeared on the mezzanine level above and padded down the circular iron staircase from the apartment's upstairs floor. In nothing but a pair of shorts and a T-shirt, with his hair sleep-roughened and his jaw covered in dark stubble, it was obvious the doorbell had woken him.

The buzz in Carmel's abdomen turned to a hum as he scrubbed his hands down his face before walking past her hiding place to the apartment's front door.

Her gaze fixed on his back as he began the process of unlocking the several different latches on the huge iron door and the dog's barks became frenzied.

The worn T-shirt stretched over defined muscles, accentuating the impressive breadth of his shoulders. Carmel's gaze followed the line of his spine to the tight muscles of his glutes, displayed to perfection in stretchy black boxers.

Then he opened the door and all hell broke loose.

Surprise turned to complete astonishment as a large, floppy dog bounded into the room, its toenails scratching on the expensive flooring, its barks turning to ecstatic yips.

'Hey, boy, you missed me?' Ross said, his

deep voice rough as the animal jumped to place its gigantic paws on his chest. What breed was that exactly?

A smaller person would surely have been bowled over by the dog's enthusiastic greeting, but Ross braced against the onslaught, obviously used to the frenzied hello, and managed to hold his ground as the huge hound lavished him with slobbering affection.

Ross De Courtney has a dog? Seriously?

She waited, expecting him to discipline the dog, but instead he rubbed its ears and a deep rusty laugh could be heard under the dog's barking.

'Relax, Rocky,' he said, eventually grabbing the dog's collar and managing to wrestle it back onto all fours. 'Now, sit, boy,' he said, with all the strident authority of a Fortune 500 Company CEO. The dog gave him a goofy grin and ignored him, its whole body wagging backwards and forwards with the force of its joy.

'Rocky, sit!' The incisive command was delivered by a small middle-aged woman dressed in dungarees and biker boots—her Afro hair expertly tied back in a multi-coloured scarf—who must have brought the dog and followed it into the apartment.

The dog instantly dropped its butt, although the goofy grin remained fixed on Ross as if he were the most wonderful person in the known universe.

'How the heck do you do that, Nina?' Ross murmured, sounding disgruntled as the woman produced a treat and patted the dog's head.

Carmel grinned, feeling almost as goofy as the dog, her astonishment at the animal's appearance turning into a warm glow.

Ross De Courtney has a dog who adores him.

'Practice,' the dog trainer said as she unloaded a bowl, a blanket and a lead from her backpack. After dropping them on the kitchen counter, she gave the dog a quick scratch behind the ears before heading back towards the door. 'You've gotta show him who's boss, Ross. Not just tell him.'

'Right,' Ross replied, still endearingly disgruntled. 'I thought I was.'

'Uh-huh.' The woman snorted, her knowing smile more than a little sceptical. 'Dogs are smart, they know when someone's just playing at being a badass.'

They had a brief conversation about plans for the coming week—Nina was obviously his regular dog walker and sitter and had been looking after Rocky while Ross was out of the country—before the woman left.

Carmel stood watching from behind the door to her room, aware she was eavesdropping again, but unable to stop herself. A bubble of hope swelled under her breastbone right next to the warm glow as she observed Ross interact with his devoted pet. Talking in a firm, steady voice, he calmed the animal down, rewarded him every time he did as he was told, and fed and watered him, before pouring himself a mug of coffee and tipping a large helping of psychedelic cereal into a bowl. The rapport between Ross and the animal—which Carmel eventually decided was some kind of haphazard cross between a wolfhound and a Labrador—was unmistakable once the dog stretched out its lumbering limbs over the expensive rug in the centre of the living area for a nap.

Questions bombarded her. How old was the dog? How long had it been his? Where had he got it? Because it looked like some kind of rescue dog. Definitely a mongrel crossbreed and not at all the sort of expensive pedigree status symbol she would expect a man in his position to own if he owned a pet at all. Especially a man who had insisted he didn't do emotional attachments.

The bubble of hope became painful.

Maybe it was the jet lag, or the emotional hit of her earlier conversation with Mac, or simply the weird disconnect of being so far away from home—and so far outside her comfort zone— with a man who still had the power to make her ache after all these years… But this discovery felt significant. And also strangely touching.

That Ross De Courtney not only had a softer side he hadn't told her about. But one he'd actively refused to acknowledge.

Ross gave a huge yawn, and raked his fingers through his hair, carving the thick chestnut mass into haphazard rows.

The swell of emotion sharpened into something much more immediate. And the hum in her abdomen returned, to go with the warm glow. She cleared her throat loudly, determined to ignore it.

Ross's head lifted, and his gaze locked on her.

The heat climbed into her cheeks and bottomed out in her stomach.

'You're up early,' he said, the curt, frustrated tone unmistakable. 'How long have you been standing there?'

The easy camaraderie he'd shown the dog had disappeared, along with his relaxed demeanour. He had morphed back into the brooding billionaire again—guarded and suspicious and watchful.

The only problem was, it was harder to pull off while he was seated on a bar stool in his shorts with a bowl of the sort of sugary cereal Mac would consider a major treat. She'd seen a glimpse of the man who existed behind the mask now and it had given her hope.

She walked into the room, brutally aware a second too late she hadn't changed out of her own sleep attire when his gaze skimmed over her bare legs—could he tell she wasn't wearing a bra? The visceral surge of heat soared.

But she forced herself to keep on walking. Not to back down, not to apologise, and most of all to keep the conversation where it needed to be.

'Long enough,' she said. 'So just answer me this, Ross. You have the capacity to love Rocky here.' The dog's ears pricked up at the sound of his name and he bounded towards her. She laughed at the animal's greeting, surprised but also pleased to see that up close he was an even uglier dog than she'd realised, one ear apparently chewed off, his snout scarred and his eyes two different colours—one murky brown, the other murky grey. 'But you don't have the capacity to love your own child? Is that the way of it?'

'It's hardly the same thing,' Ross managed, furious she had spied on him, but even more furious at the spike of arousal as his houseguest bent forward to give Rocky's stomach a generous rub and her breasts swayed under soft cotton. 'A dog is not a child,' he added, trying to keep his mind on the conversation, and his irritation. And not the surge of desire working its way south.

He'd stayed at work until late in the evening last night, catching up on emails and doing conference calls with some of De Courtney's Asian offices precisely so he could avoid this sort of scenario. He'd had plans to be out today as soon as Nina dropped off Rocky, but he'd overslept. And now here they were, both virtually naked with only a goofy dog to keep them sane. While he'd missed his pet, Rocky wasn't doing a damn thing to stop the heat swelling in his groin.

'I know, but surely the ability to care and nurture is not that different,' she said as he tried to keep track of the conversation and not the way her too short nightwear gave him a glimpse of her panties as she bent over—and made her bare, toned legs look about a mile long. 'All I'm saying is if you have the capacity to care for Rocky here, why wouldn't you have the capacity to care for Mac?' she said, scratching his dog's head vigorously and laughing when Rocky collapsed on the floor to display his stomach for a scratch—like the great big attention junkie he was.

Heck, Rocky, show a bit of restraint, why don't you?

'Hey, boy, you like that, don't you?' she said, still chuckling, the throaty sound playing havoc with his control. The dog's eyes became dazed with pleasure.

He knew how Rocky felt as he watched her

breasts under the loose T-shirt—which shouldn't have looked seductive, but somehow was more tantalising than the most expensive lingerie.

Is she even wearing a bra?

The dog's tongue flopped out of the side of its mouth as it panted its approval, in seventh heaven now from the vigorous stomach rub.

Terrific, now he was jealous of his own dog.

He remained perched on the stool, grateful for the breakfast bar, which was hiding the strength of his own reaction.

She finished rubbing Rocky's belly, patted the animal and then rose, to fix that inquisitive gaze back on him. The forthright consideration in her bright blue eyes only made him more uncomfortable and on edge. Almost as if she could see inside him, to something that wasn't there… Or rather, something that he certainly did not intend to acknowledge.

'You didn't answer my question,' she said as she walked towards the breakfast bar.

He kept his gaze on her face, so as not to increase the torture by dwelling on the way the T-shirt barely skimmed her bottom.

When exactly had he become a leg man, as well as a breast man, by the way?

She perched on the stool opposite, hiding her legs at last.

This was precisely why he hadn't wanted to have her in his condo. Intrusive questions were bad enough, but the feel of his control slipping was far worse.

She cleared her throat.

'What was the question again?' he asked, because he'd totally lost the thread of the conversation.

'If you can form an attachment to Rocky, why would you think you can't form one to Mac?' she repeated, the flush on her cheeks suggesting she knew exactly where his mind had wandered. Why did that only make the insistent heat worse?

He took a mouthful of his Lucky Charms and chewed slowly, to give himself time to get his mind out of his shorts and form a coherent and persuasive argument.

He swallowed. 'A child requires a great deal more attention than a dog,' he murmured. 'And Nina spends almost as much time with Rocky as I do. Because I happen to be a workaholic.'

It was the truth.

He didn't have much of a social life, and that was the way he liked it. When he'd first taken over the reins of De Courtney's after his father's death he had resented the time and trouble it had taken to drag the ailing company into the twenty-first century, but he'd soon discovered he found the work rewarding. And he was good at it. Especially undoing all the harm his father had done with his autocratic and regressive approach to recruitment and training, not to mention innovation. The fact the bastard would be turning in his grave at all the changes Ross had made to De Courtney's archaic management structures was another fringe benefit. He'd never enjoyed socialising that much and had only attended those events where he needed to be seen. He had no family except Katie and he'd hardly spoken to her in years, and he had very few friends in New York—just a couple of guys he shared the occasional beer or squash game with. It was one of the reasons he'd moved to the US—he preferred his solitude and as much anonymity as he could have at the head of an international logistics conglomerate. And that just left his sex life, which he had always been careful to keep ruthlessly separate from other parts of his life.

All of which surely meant he wasn't cut out to be a father. No matter how easily he had bonded with Rocky, after finding the pup beaten and crying in a dumpster behind the apartment two summers ago. And he'd made a spur-of-the-moment decision to keep him.

But that hardly made him good parent material, not even close.

'That's true,' Carmel said, and nodded. 'A child does need your full attention at least some of the time. And I've already figured out how dedicated you are to your job.'

Something hollow pulsed in his chest, right alongside the surge of desire that would not die.

'I also live in New York, which would mean any time I could give Mac would be limited,' he added, determined to press home the point—despite the hole forming in his chest.

Her pensive look faded, and her lips curved upward, the blue of her irises brightening to a rich sapphire. The hollow sensation turned to something raw and compelling.

'Do you know? That's the first time you've called Mac by his name,' she said, her voice fierce, and scarily rich with hope.

'Is it?' he said, staring back at her, absorbing the shock to his system as he struggled not to react to her smile.

Good grief, the woman was even more stunning when she smiled. That open and forthright expression of pure uninhibited joy was a lethal weapon… How could he have forgotten the devastating effect her spontaneous smile had had on him once before? The driving need to please her, to hear her laugh, something that had effectively derailed all his common sense four years ago.

He'd known it would be dangerous bringing her here. But the hit to his libido was nowhere near as concerning as the chasm opening up in his chest at the first sign of her approval.

'I think it's a very positive sign,' she said.

'I wouldn't read too much into it if I were

you,' he said, trying to counter her excitement. But even he could hear the defensiveness in his voice.

Where was that coming from?

He didn't need her approval, or anyone's. He didn't need validation, or permission for the way he had chosen to live his life—avoiding forming the kind of emotional attachments she was speaking about. That hollow ache meant nothing. He'd stopped needing that kind of validation as a boy, when he'd discovered at a very young age his father didn't love him—and never would. That he was simply a means to an end. He didn't consider it a weakness, he considered it a strength. Because as soon as he'd finally accepted the truth, he'd worked on becoming emotionally self-sufficient.

And, okay, maybe Rocky had sneaked under his guard. But he didn't have room for any more emotional commitments. Why couldn't she accept that?

He opened his mouth to say exactly that, but before he could say any of it she said, 'You haven't said whether you want to be a father or not. Just that you can't be one.'

'I had a vasectomy when I was twenty-one,' he said, but even he could hear the cop-out in his answer. 'I think that speaks for itself.'

'Does it?' she said, far too astute for her own good, looking at him again with that forthright

...pression that suggested she could see right into his soul… A soul he'd spent a lifetime protecting from exactly this kind of examination, a soul that suddenly felt transparent and exposed. 'Because I'd say your reasons for having that vasectomy are what's really important, and you haven't explained them to me.'

'I didn't want to be a father,' he said flatly, but the lie felt heavy on his tongue, because she was right. It had never been about whether or not he *wanted* to be a father. He'd never even asked himself that question. It had always been much more basic than that. It had always been about not wanting to get a woman pregnant.

She crossed her arms over her chest, looking momentarily stricken by his answer. But then her gaze softened again. 'But now you are one, how do you feel about Mac?'

'Responsible. And terrified,' he said, surprising himself by blurting out the truth.

'Terrified? Why?' she pushed. The bright sheen of hope and excitement in her gaze—as if she'd made some important breakthrough, as if she had found something he knew wasn't there—only disturbing him more.

'That I'll do to him what my father did to me,' he said. 'And his father did to him. There's a legacy in the De Courtney family that no child should have to be any part of,' he said, determined to shut down the conversation.

that he could see her generous breasts and that marvelous bump, but all the rest of her, too. Her delicate shoulders, her lovely legs.

She was beautiful. She always had been, but today it was on display.

"Did you find a hairbrush in your bathroom suite?" he asked mildly.

Nina glared at him but straightened her shoulders. "I might as well marry you as not, I suppose."

"I'm touched," he said. "Deeply."

He did not rise from the small table where he took his breakfast. The expansive windows let the sun in, and he liked to bask in it while he sipped at an espresso and tracked various items of interest in the financial pages. Only after this ritual did he venture into his actual office, where he spent more and more of his time since his father's decline these last months had forced the reluctant Cronos to shift the bulk of his duties to his son. Zeus had gone to great lengths to make himself seem ineffectual—as if the kingdom ran itself. If anyone outside the palace even knew he had an office, they assumed it was a PR affair kept on hand for no other purpose than to clean up the messes he made.

He had one of those, too. But that wasn't what he did all day.

Another thing he did not intend to share.

Zeus waved Nina into the seat opposite him and then leaned back to give off his usual impression of an indolent little princeling. The one she already thought he was. So she could truly contemplate the step she was taking.

Nina took her time sitting down, and he couldn't tell if her discomfort came from him—or the fact that she'd proven his point by effectively unveiling herself. And he liked his games, it was true. But it was untenable that she should sit with him in *discomfort*.

"The first time I noticed you was at an opera some years ago," he said, though he would have sworn he had no such memory. That she had been there, like wallpaper, until he'd decided to use her as a weapon to effect his escape. Yet it seemed he could remember that night in Vienna with perfect clarity. "You sat just behind me, and I did not hear a note. All I could think was that you smelled of strawberries."

"That's because I was eating them," Nina replied in that bland way of hers. Her lips twitched. "Dipped in chocolate, naturally, or what's the point? Perhaps you were hungry."

He lifted his espresso to his lips and took a sip. "It fascinates me that you will not take a compliment."

"While it fascinates me that you're so determined to give them." She lifted a shoulder. "I don't need to be complimented by you, Zeus. The fact of the matter is that if I were choosing husbands, I would not choose you, either."

"I'm devastated. And you are still trapped. My condolences on the life of hardship that awaits you here."

But she'd settled into her chair, despite his sardonic tone. And was clearly leaning into this topic. "You're selfish. Your behavior is atrocious. That's on a good day. As far as anyone can tell, the main purpose of your existence appears to be racking up as many sexual encounters as you can and flaunting them in the tabloids."

"You say that like it's a bad thing."

Nina sighed. "As far as I'm aware, marriages like these survive because certain understandings are put in place from the start."

She was more correct than she knew, but

Zeus did not let himself react. He bit back the automatic response that leaped in him. And waited until he was calm enough to shrug.

With all expected indolence.

"I cannot say I have concerned myself overmuch with the state of marriages, royal or otherwise," he said.

Across from him, Nina shifted in her chair. "I know that Isabeau had every intention of continuing her usual exploits while married to you. She talked about it all the time. All she needed to do was pop out an heir and then, duty done, she could return to doing what she truly enjoyed. The expectation was that you would do the same. And that neither of you would care."

"And am I to expect the same understanding with you?" he asked. "Or are you worried that's what I want?"

He forced himself to sound bored when he was…not. He unclenched his jaw. And his fist. And did not allow himself to contemplate this woman with other lovers. The very idea made everything in him…burn.

Not that Nina noticed.

"Oh, no, you misunderstand," she said airily. "I already know my part."

Everything in Zeus went still. Dangerously still.

Alarmingly still, even. Had he been paying attention to anything but her, he might have heeded those alarms.

"I beg your pardon. Do you have some lover you feel you cannot give up?"

Because if she did, he would rip the man apart. And then the world.

He opted not to ask himself why he, who had always professed he could not begin to understand the notion of jealousy or possession, felt both here. To a disturbing degree.

"It's not about *me*," Nina said, frowning at him. "It's for you. I want you to go out there and do whatever it is you do so that I don't have to worry about it."

There was no answer she could have given that would have stunned him more.

"So you don't…have to *worry* about it?" He could do little more than blink in astonishment.

She nodded enthusiastically. "It's a perfect solution. I'm sure your sexual demands are very… Well. *Demanding*. And I certainly couldn't keep up with all that." Nina waved a hand. "You should go out there and keep spreading it around, the way you always have. You have my blessing."

And that strange temper kicked through him all over again. Laced through with what he could only assume was outrage that this woman who would be his wife was offering him carte blanche to carry on as if he were to remain single.

It felt blistering. Life-altering.

Yet the strangest part was, he knew that what she was suggesting should have thrilled him. Zeus had never been any particular fan of monogamy. He had often advanced the theory that it didn't truly exist. That it was only fear masquerading as all the pledging of troths and other such horrors.

He should have been delighted with this, and yet he was not.

Not at all.

"This way, everyone's happy," she was saying brightly. *Happily.* "You can do what you do best. And I—"

"What is it, pray, that you do best?" Zeus growled. "I shudder to think."

Nina cast a look his way that suggested he was being strange. "I don't know what I do best. I've never had the opportunity to find out." But she studied him for moment, tilting her head to one side. "I thought you'd be thrilled. You do not look thrilled."

"You're awfully quick to forgo the pleasures of the flesh, Nina."

She laughed, which was somehow the most insulting thing yet. "I think I'll survive."

"Will you?"

And he didn't mean to move. Zeus would have sworn that he'd had no intention of doing anything of the sort.

But then, as if he had no part in it, his hand was reaching out. And then he was leaning across the small table until he could hook his palm around her neck.

And then pull her face to his.

He could taste her startled exhalation. He could see the shock in those warm, pretty brown eyes.

And everything about her was sweet. Soft.

But he kissed her like a drowning man, all the same.

Hot and hard, like he was setting a fire, then throwing gasoline on the blaze.

And it was like the six months that he knew had existed between that night with her and now simply…disappeared. As if they'd been shadows that he'd traveled through and nothing more.

Because this, finally, was vivid.

It was *right*.

It was the opposite of boring.

Without lifting his mouth from hers, Zeus moved from his seat, rounding the small table so he could lift her up and pull her into his arms. And she fit differently, with that beautiful belly between them, but somehow that only made it hotter.

They had made a child, and he could feel the solid weight of the baby between them, and still she kissed him with all of that passion, all of that need, that had haunted him for half a year.

Maybe it had haunted her, too.

He kissed her and he kissed her, deeper and wilder with every stroke, until he got his answer.

Then he kept on kissing her, until he'd almost forgotten that he was marrying her for any reason but this.

This slick perfection. This unnerving sense that he was home at last.

That thought sobered him too quickly. This was about a narrative, that was all, and he needed to be in control of it. He needed to make sure she was seen the way he wanted her seen. The same way he made sure he was seen in only one way outside his office. *Home* had nothing to do with this. Zeus didn't know what the word meant.

He pulled back so he could rest his forehead on hers, letting one hand move down to stroke the belly between them at last.

Because he knew every other part of her. He remembered it all. In extraordinary detail.

Her eyes were closed, and she was breathing heavily. It took her a long time to look at him again, and when she did, she looked dazed.

"That can't happen again," she told him, very distinctly.

But all he could do was stand there, sharing breath with her while his sex shouted at him and every part of him urged him to get closer. To keep going. To do whatever was necessary to have her naked and beneath him, sobbing out her joy as they found each other again—

"Zeus." Her voice cracked a little on his name. "This *can't* happen again. Ever."

"Somehow, little hen," he murmured, reaching up to slide his hand along her pink-tinged cheek and brush his thumb over her lips, "I think that it will."

When she pulled away, he let her. Just as he let her rush from out of the room. But he could taste her on his mouth again. At last. He could feel the press of her body against his, like she'd marked him.

And he found himself smiling long after she'd gone.

CHAPTER FIVE

THAT KISS COMPLICATED EVERYTHING.

It was bad enough that Nina had agreed to marry him. She'd lain awake that first night, staring at the ornate ceiling that arched high above her. She'd listened to the sound of the sea outside. And she'd asked herself what on earth she thought she was doing here.

But came back, always, to her baby.

How could she reasonably refuse to marry her baby's father? She'd argued with herself all night. Because certainly, she had her issues with royals in general. This child would be a crown prince or princess. Nina had never met one of those she didn't have deep suspicions about in one way or another, but that didn't mean there couldn't be a perfectly lovely version.

Was that good enough reason to deny her child its birthright?

The fact of the matter was, she wasn't romantic, despite the odd daydream. Not really. She had congratulated herself on that, lying in that vast bed in her guest bedchamber, running her fingers up and down her sides and over her belly as she tried to get used to sleeping on one side or the other.

I can make decisions based on what's good for you, she told her baby. *Not silly little fairy tales of true love.*

She might have dreamed of romance and other such things when she was with Isabeau, but that was only because the Haught Montagne court had been devoid of any such tender notions. And because she'd been sixteen when she'd first gotten there and might have been foolish enough to think *what if* in those first few months. Before Isabeau had stopped pretending and had showed her true colors. When Nina had let herself imagine that there might be a place she belonged.

Her years at Isabeau's side had cured her of such foolishness. And watching Isabeau's many passionate entanglements—all while she was so determined to marry Zeus—had soured Nina on romance completely. Zeus's own exploits, extensively covered in the press, had suggested to her that love was nothing more than a cynical bid to sell more column space in greedy magazines.

Nina had always told herself that when she was finally set free, she would go out into the world and follow her heart wherever it led without involving the tabloids at all.

But what she'd discovered was that she liked following her heart well enough— but only in terms of the many destinations she could finally explore on her own terms. She'd never had any interest in following her heart to *people*. Not once in her first two months of travel, before she'd started to feel so wretched, had it even occurred to her to try out a *passionate entanglement* of her own. Maybe she should have.

She'd loved what little part she'd taken in the happy nights in the various hostels where she'd stayed. It had seemed like such a different world, all these heedless young people, dancing and drinking without a care—night after night, as if no one was watching them. Because no one *was* watching them.

But she'd never followed through on any

of the invitations, spoken or unspoken, that had come her way.

A romantic would have, surely. A romantic would have wondered *what if.*

That had been what decided her. If she was the kind of woman who intended to hold out for love, that would have been one thing. But she wasn't. She was practical. A realist. Love was for silly girls in skimpy dresses, filled with wonder and maybes. Not grown, weathered women who knew better, who'd already been called a horrid disgrace in at least ten languages. And if she wasn't the sort who was going to hold out for romantic love, she might as well marry the Prince, who had his own, likely nefarious, reasons for marrying her—but what did that matter?

It was about her child in the end.

That was the only love that mattered.

She'd marched off to find him that morning, filled with a sense of purpose and even pleasure that she could secure her child's future like this. Almost as if, finally, she'd relegated her memories of her own cold, hard childhood to the dustbin.

Then Zeus had kissed her and ruined everything.

Because now she was forced to lie in her bed, night after night, and wonder if the reason she hadn't used her travel time to experiment in all the ways everyone else did was not because she was so practical and *above it all*.

She was terribly afraid it had been because of him.

After all, she'd only started on that adventure in the first place because of her night in Prince Zeus's arms. And once the scandal had broken, she had happily left Haught Montagne. Then marched out into the world, telling herself with every step that she barely remembered a thing, because all that really mattered was that she was free of Isabeau at last.

But even if that were true—and it wasn't—his kiss brought it all back.

Because the man tasted like sunshine and the darkest nights, sin and sweet surrender, and she remembered every single thing she'd ever done with him. Every last detail of that long, languorous night. Almost as if his betrayal of her come morning didn't matter.

Now she was more than six months pregnant, trapped in the Palace of the Gods with the only man she'd ever met who could reasonably suggest he might earn that title in the modern world. And Prince Zeus, the wickedest man alive, was insisting she marry him.

Nina couldn't come up with a good enough reason why she shouldn't.

But she'd regretted it the moment she said she would.

Not just because he'd kissed her—and she'd betrayed herself entirely by kissing him back like a desperate woman, a shocking truth she was still struggling to come to terms with—but because the palace staff descended upon her soon after, the inevitable Theosian courtiers in their wake.

And as they began to play their little games around her, it occurred to Nina that she hadn't even thought to have *this* nightmare.

"I can't have a staff and all those horrible aristocratic groupies," she told Zeus one night at another one of the dinners he insisted upon. Tonight he wore a crisp linen affair that would have melted into a tragedy of wrinkles on anyone else in this climate. On Zeus, it did not dare.

It seemed at odds with the man she'd glimpsed in his offices earlier that same day, when she'd been wandering about on one of her art walks, looking…focused and somber as he spoke in low tones with his ministers, none of them the least bit groupie-ish. Almost as if he took his job seriously when no one was watching him.

She didn't know where to put that. Particularly when he showed up looking every inch his rakish, playboy self.

"Some of the aristocratic groupies you disdain are my cousins, Nina," he replied, genially enough. But she was sure she could see behind that mask of his. Maybe more than she should.

"They are a pit of snakes, waiting to strike."

Zeus laughed. "Fair enough. But you cannot hate a snake for merely following its nature."

"I can choose not to put myself in striking distance." He only gazed at her, and she blew out a breath. "The last thing in the world I want is a set of my own courtiers. They're already circling around me, looking for a head to bite off."

"They are no match for you, little hen."

Another ecstatic sunset was stretched out behind him, framing him in deep pinks and oranges. And Nina's pulse was too quick, another betrayal, suggesting as it did that she was *afraid* when she was not. Why should she be afraid? What were a pack of status-hungry aristocrats to her?

But her pulse carried on making her a liar.

"Perhaps it is not the sad reality of palace courtiers that you dislike," Zeus said, almost as if he was addressing the sunset instead of her. "Here they do not creep about the palace at all hours, as in Haught Montagne. They are only allowed in at my discretion. Perhaps what you cannot fathom is facing them without your usual armor."

"I don't know what you mean," Nina threw back at him.

Even as her stomach dropped and her pulse picked up again. Because she did know. One of the reasons she hadn't minded all those terrible articles about her was because…they weren't about her, really. They were about the character she'd played to annoy Isabeau. Or even, in some cases, about the ungainly orphan girl no one had ever wanted. That was also not her, because she'd wanted her own parents, not new ones. After a certain point, she'd taken pleasure in being overlooked.

She'd hidden herself her whole life, but not here.

Here, she dressed as if she considered herself just as pretty as any idle aristocratic courtier whose job it was to look lovely at all times. She did her hair and took care with her appearance for the first time in her life. And yes, she was doing it because Zeus had challenged her. Because he'd suggested she couldn't handle showing herself.

But she hadn't expected how much she would hate the fact that the sort of people she disliked most could see her, too.

"Nina."

She only kept herself from jolting by the barest thread. And that was before he reached over and took her hand, sending that rush of heat and longing shooting through her, lighting her up. Everywhere.

His gaze was intent. "Hiding in the way you have may have amused you, but it also gave them ammunition. Imagine if you denied them even that. It is possible to keep a boundary around what is private, what is yours, without playing at dress-up."

"Is that what you do?" she managed to ask. And she knew she'd scored a point when that gaze of his shuttered. Behind him, the winter sun dipped below the horizon. Zeus let go of her hand.

Nina had the distinct thought that, perhaps, she was tired of point scoring.

But that felt far too much like an admission of something she refused to accept, so she swept it aside and attended to yet another spectacular feast laid out before her.

"Whatever you think of courtiers, you must choose a staff," Zeus said after a moment or two. In his usual manner, all ease and male grace and that wickedness beneath. "Not for your personal needs, as I am sure you will tell me you can take care of yourself, but because you will be Queen one day. And there will be a great many considerations it is better a staff handles. I think you know this."

Her hand was still branded by his touch. Her body was still reacting to that jolt of its favorite source of heat. And Nina wanted to argue, or maybe succumb to the pressure inside her that felt too much like a sob—but Zeus had that look in those gleaming green eyes of his again. That wicked, knowing light when she was determined that no more kissing would occur.

Because when he kissed her, she couldn't think straight.

Nina couldn't have that. She was a practical, rational, capable woman. She would not allow *kisses* to sidetrack her.

Even if kissing Zeus again was all she thought about some days.

To her eternal shame.

Zeus made himself scarce at certain hours of the day. And now and again she saw him as he apparently tended to the actual business of running his country, which was clearly a secret. Maybe the biggest secret, certainly outside the palace walls, and one she clearly didn't know how to process. Nina decided that instead of processing any of these things about him that didn't fit—or picking courtiers she didn't want or staff she didn't trust—she would dedicate herself to what she did best, instead.

That meant she hid in the palace library and reveled not only in the books but in the fact that no one questioned her right to sit around and read as much as she liked about whatever she liked. Or to sit in a window seat and daydream. No one came to lecture her. No one demanded she attend them. No one punished her if she wandered off by herself for hours.

Daphne learned quickly to track her down in the stacks, where Nina could always be found sitting with her feet up, a book open in her lap.

If she didn't look too closely at her situation, she almost felt free.

Or at least off on the sort of holiday she'd always longed to take after she finished seeing the world.

But on the first morning of her second week in Theosia, Daphne hurried her through her breakfast, then told her there would be no library time today.

"Library time is the only thing keeping me sane," Nina told her aide—who she had made the head of her staff. They had both stared at each other, then nodded, and that had been that. Painless, really.

"I have faith in your sanity," Daphne replied. "In or out of the palace library."

And then delivered her to the airfield, where liveried servants waited to escort her onto a waiting plane. Zeus was already there, reclining in a leather seat as if it was a throne. Or as if he wanted her to think it was.

"Where are we going?" she asked as she sat down in one of the bucket seats, aiming a smile at the hovering air steward. She declined refreshment, her gaze on the man across from her. And the way he looked at her, all that dark green heat.

"I've spent the week planning how we will reveal ourselves to the world," he said when the steward was gone.

"Reveal ourselves?" Nina didn't like the sound of that at all. "I don't know what you mean. You are overrevealed as it is, surely. There was a swimsuit edition of you only last month."

"I do look fantastic in a swimsuit," he said, as if she'd been lavishing him with praise.

Nina could only roll her eyes. Because he was right. He did.

"Come now," Zeus chided her, his mouth curving. He propped up his head and all that dark blond hair with one hand. "You cannot possibly imagine that you can turn up out of the blue, hugely pregnant with the child of a prince, and reveal nothing about how you came to find yourself in this state. Especially when that prince is me. And then, of course, we have decided to marry. It will need announcing."

"I don't see why."

He only smiled. "You do. You don't want to see why, but you do. It will be reported on either way. Better to attempt to control the narrative."

"Alternatively, we could try just going about our lives," Nina said dryly. "I think the world would catch on, narrative or no narrative."

"You worked for Isabeau for far too long not to know how this works," Zeus said, too much laughter in his gaze. Mocking laughter, she thought. "You know this game as well as I do. Why are you pretending you don't know how to play?"

She tried to ignore the way her pulse rocketed around, because it had nothing to do with anything. It was proximity, that was all. Maybe it was biology. Maybe a pregnant woman couldn't help herself from feeling this way in the presence of her child's father. Maybe the need to want him was in her bones.

But that didn't mean she planned to surrender to it, either.

She tried to think strategically, the way she would if she had a little more distance from the scenario. The scenario being a wicked prince who looked at her as if he wanted nothing more than to taste her. If she were Zeus, what would she do? And why would it require a trip?

And he was right. She did know.

"You're staging some kind of engagement scene," she said after a moment or two. "You want to start them all talking about us again."

She almost said *on your terms*, but she remembered herself. The last time they'd been talked about had been on his terms, too. The only difference this time was that he was telling her what he was doing in advance.

Nina was tempted to feel a bit of outrage about that but couldn't. Because the way his smile broke across his face felt like a reward, and it made everything in her...shift. Then roll.

Then keep right on rolling until it became a molten, hot brand between her legs.

"Very good, little hen," he said.

And God, the way he said that. *Little hen.* It shouldn't be allowed.

Her breasts seemed to press against the

fabric of her dress. She had to tell herself, sternly, not to squirm in her seat. It would only make things worse.

"I don't know what makes you think you can call me that," she said, because she was reeling. And because she was desperate for some hint of equilibrium. "You do know that Isabeau called me that as an insult, don't you?"

"It's different when I say it."

It wasn't as if there was ever a moment in Zeus's presence when his arrogance didn't seem to take over the room. Or the taxiing plane, in this case. But every now and again, it seemed to boil inside of her. "How is it different?"

"Because you like it when I say it, Nina."

And suddenly, it was as if he had gripped her between his hands and was squeezing tight, forcing all the breath from her body.

All she could think about was kissing him. Hurling herself from her seat and finding his mouth with hers. The wild longing seemed to expand within her, crowding out any possibility of anything else, even breath—

You need to stop, she ordered herself. *Now.* Nina made a little show of rubbing her belly and murmuring to the baby, who was fast asleep inside her. And then wondered if that was the kind of mother she was going to be. The kind who shamelessly used her own child to get out of awkward moments of her own creation.

"Why do you look sad?" Zeus demanded, still lounging there as the plane began to gather steam along the runway. "Surely you cannot be so distraught over the use of a nickname."

"First, I can be distraught about anything I wish," Nina retorted. "Whether you like it or not. But I was thinking about motherhood."

Their gazes seemed to tangle then, and suddenly everything seemed…stark. Stripped down in ways she wasn't sure they had ever been before—not since that night. Not since they stayed awake as the hours grew narrower and told each other things that could only belong in moments like that.

Stolen. Illicit. Never to be repeated.

She had no doubt, as the plane leaped from the earth, that Zeus was remembering the very same thing.

Are you lonely? she had dared to whisper, there in his vast guest rooms in the old Haught

Montagne castle. A far cry from where she lived, down in the servants' quarters.

He had held her beside him, pulled fast to his side because they had not let each other go all night, but he did not laugh. The look he gave her was…quizzical.

What would make you ask such a thing of me? I'm forever surrounded by people. I could not be lonely if I tried.

An orphanage is filled with people, she'd replied. *And yet it is the loneliest place on earth.*

He had looked at her for a long time, still not smiling, so she had no choice but to notice how truly beautiful he really was. All those sculpted lines. That heartbreakingly sensual mouth. *Princes do not believe in loneliness*, he had said.

She had traced his cheek, his jaw, with her fingers. She had wanted to remember this, remember him, with everything she was. *I don't think it works that way.*

He had rolled her over to her back, setting himself over her again, and already she had been soft and ready for him. It was as if, after that first impossible kiss, he had made her body his.

And she had loved it.

Yes, he had whispered harshly. His green eyes glittered. *I am always lonely.*

And then he had thrust deep inside her, and she had stopped doing anything so difficult as forming words.

Now, Nina was glad they were on a plane. And that takeoff was a distraction. And that she could fuss around with the new maternity outfit she wore, one of the many items of clothing that had appeared in her bedchamber over the last week. She'd gone and looked for the clothes she'd come with, only to find them missing.

I will be certain to take it up with the palace laundry, my lady, Daphne had said mildly enough. *But who can say when I'll be able to speak to them? You had better wear these things in the meantime.*

Nina hadn't had any doubt whose order it was to dress her differently, but still. She thought she ought to protest. She ought to put up *some* resistance, surely. But the look of pleasure and heat in Zeus's gaze the next time he saw her in something that accentuated her new curves…did something to her.

A bit of acid stomach, perhaps, she told

herself tartly as the plane hit cruising altitude and the man across from her was still lounging there as if propped up by indolence instead of his own arm.

And she thought, with great clarity, that discussing the moment they'd had at takeoff might actually kill her.

"What is it you do when you disappear all day?" she asked instead, though she suspected she knew. As impossible as it was to imagine this man doing anything virtuous—or even vaguely responsible. "I would have thought debauching virgins was something you had down to a science, requiring very little time. And more to the point, I did think most of your trysts occurred at night."

He treated her to one of those smiles of his, wolfish and edgy, a perfect match for the heat in his green gaze and the echoing blast of fire deep inside her.

"I don't think you really want to know."

"You don't have to tell me, of course," Nina said with a shrug. "After all, ours will be two very separate lives."

She didn't think she was imagining the way his jaw tightened at that. "I don't know that either one of us has the faintest idea what our lives will be like. But we were speaking of motherhood, were we not?"

"Indeed we were." She felt as if she'd dodged a hard punch there, or maybe caught it, because her breath seemed to come a little quicker. "I don't remember my mother, you see. Not really. I have vague impressions of a kind voice, a hand on my cheek. Though I can't say that those are actual memories. They might just as easily be things I thought I ought to imagine. Some of the kids at the orphanage could remember everything, back to when they were in a cot, staring up at their parents. But not me. You lost your mother, too, did you not?"

He was still lounging, but somehow, he looked more like a predator set to pounce than he did relaxed in any way. "I did. I was eleven."

Nina nodded. "Then you remember more."

Still, he didn't move. "I do."

The prickle of some kind of warning moved over her then, though she couldn't have said what it was. She looked down at her bump instead, smoothing her hands over the soft, stretchy material that somehow managed to both emphasize her pregnancy and make her look more delicate at the same time. It shocked her how much she liked it, when she'd spent so many years concealing anything real about herself—loath as she was to admit it. Not only choosing the most unflattering clothes, but wearing them two sizes too big, or too small, so she always looked misshapen. All for the reward of hearing Isabeau's shriek of fury every time she walked in the room.

I cannot bear the sight of you! the Princess would scream. Which meant Nina could retreat and have an afternoon to herself.

But she hadn't simply gotten used to the subterfuge—she'd liked it. And yes, maybe hid there, too. Because she hadn't changed the way she'd dressed when she'd gone traveling. She'd continued to do nothing with her appearance except make herself look worse.

This was the first time she'd tried to look pretty. And somehow, it felt important that it was with Zeus.

"I hope that I do all right," she said after a moment. "With mothering. I have no examples to look up to."

"You will be an excellent mother," he said, his voice something like rough.

And Nina didn't realize how badly she'd needed to hear those words until he said them. How she'd longed to hear someone say that to her. "I hope so," she whispered. "But it seems such a complicated thing, to raise a child. I was raised by a committee of disinterested matrons. Who knows what harm a single person might do?"

Zeus got an odd look on his beautiful face. As if she had somehow disarmed him.

"My mother was lovely," he said, his voice gruffer than she'd ever heard it before. "Being a small child in a palace is not, perhaps, the laugh riot you might imagine. But she made it fun. Everything was an adventure. We were always playing games, and looking back, that's probably because she was closer in age to me than to my father. The courtiers you hate so much were not kind to her. But that was just as well, as it meant we spent more time together. I would say that in terms of mothering, she taught me that it doesn't matter what you do as long as you make sure to do it with intention. I have lived by that ever since."

And she could tell by the look on his face that he had never said such things to another. She would be surprised if he'd ever said such a thing out loud before. Maybe because she knew he hadn't, she had the strangest urge to go to him. To move across the little space between their seats and put her hands on him. Hold him, somehow. This hard, bronze statue of a man.

But she did not dare.

He might not let her. Or worse, he would—and she would not know how to stop.

"I will do my best," she told him instead, feeling that starkness between them again. As if there was no artifice, no masks. Just the two of them.

She pressed her palms against her belly, as if already holding their child. The way she hoped she would, with love and wisdom, as long as she lived. And was surprised to discover that she was blinking back tears.

"Before we confront our deficiencies as parents," Zeus said in a low voice, "which in my case will be epic indeed, I am certain, there is the little matter of our wedding."

She didn't want to look at him. It felt too

fraught with peril. She blinked a few more times. "I already agreed."

"Your agreement was unnecessary, yet still appreciated." He only smiled, faintly, when she glared at him. "Before our wedding, we must turn our attention to presenting our relationship to the world. Our adoring public, if you will."

Nina sighed. "They will all find out soon enough. I'm sure you'll see to that personally."

Zeus made a tsking sound. "I think you know that's not quite how it works. Scandals are much easier to sort out than brand-new story lines, drip fed into the world to create a new impression of existing characters."

Nina made a low noise and directed her attention out the window, where everything was bright blue and sunny. This high above the clouds, surely no one should have to concern themselves with these concocted displays—the lives the public thought people in Zeus's position ought to be living, not the lives men like him actually lived.

"I hate all this," she said, more to the window than to him. "Constantly having to come up with these stories. Pretending to be whatever *character* it is the papers have decided I ought to play. I can see it now. *Queen Hen, clucking her way across Theosia.*"

And with her not hidden at all, but out here looking like *her.*

She shuddered.

"Nina. Please. No one will call you *hen* but me."

She looked back at him, and as ever, Zeus looked at his ease. She told herself that it was annoying, but somehow, she felt a little bit less…fluttery.

He waved a languid hand. "I only spend time with beautiful women, as you know. Therefore, it follows that the woman I marry must be the most beautiful of all."

"I think you're forgetting something," Nina said. He lifted his magnificent brows. "We already created one scandal. They already think I'm a mercenary gold digger. That was when I simply slept with my mistress's fiancé. What do you suppose they'll call me now?"

"Whatever I ask them to," he said, as if the matter was already settled, the articles already written.

She could feel the dubious look on her face.

"Is that how it works? You think you're in control of the tabloid cesspool?"

But Zeus only laughed. "Nina. We're going to tell them a love story. Don't you know? All is always forgiven with love."

CHAPTER SIX

ZEUS DIDN'T KNOW what was worse. Nina's look of outright horror at his use of the word *love*. Or the fact that he'd actually spoken of his mother.

Of his own accord.

He spent the rest of the flight to Paris being outrageous and needlessly provoking to make up for it.

Because he would rather have her looking at him the way she normally did. As if he required extreme forbearance.

It wouldn't change the fact that he wanted his father—and the rest of the world—to think that the most notorious prince in the world was head over heels in love with what was considered his worst scandal yet.

Once in the City of Light, a waiting car swept them off to his favorite hotel, a discreet affair on the Left Bank that suited both his sense of luxury and his need for discretion—but only sometimes.

"I'm surprised that the Theosian crown doesn't have property in Paris," Nina said once he told her where they were staying. When any other woman he knew would simply have sat there quietly, possibly murmured a few superlatives about both him and his choice of lodging, and tried to look appealing. Then again, Nina didn't have to *try*. "Haught Montagne maintains residences in most major cities. I thought everyone did."

"The kingdom has several residences here, in fact." He thrust his legs out before him in the back of the spacious car, slumping down a bit in his seat so he'd look as rumpled as possible. "I do not always wish to have my every move dissected by the palace."

She nodded briskly. "Because they're evil."

Zeus only sighed. "I like an enemy as much as the next person, but there's something you must remember about palace staff." He turned toward her so he could hold her gaze with his. "We are the product, and they are responsible for keeping that product in as pristine condition as they can manage. Yet the product also has all the power. So what are they meant to do?"

Her gaze was steady on his. "You think of yourself as a product?"

And he kept finding himself in moments like these with her. Perilously close to being his real self around this woman when he liked to pretend he couldn't even recall that he'd ever had a real self to begin with.

"I know exactly who I am," he replied.

Possibly with a touch too much heat.

"But—" Nina began, frowning.

"I cannot speak for other palaces, but I know that I give my own nothing but trouble. And yet they manage it all magnificently." He lifted a brow. "I'm surprised that a woman elevated from the orphanage, and with such a chip on her shoulder to match, would not care for the plight of honest, hardworking servants."

She let out a small sound and looked down at her belly. Then rubbed it the way she did when she was avoiding him. He found it more fascinating every time he saw her do it. And adorable.

Because he was impossible to ignore.

"I don't really think it fair that you are utterly shameless yet think you can go about shaming others," Nina said after a moment.

He bit back a smile. "Courtiers, on the other hand. Truly the dregs of humanity. I fully agree."

"You have more courtiers than a picnic has ants."

"They like to froth about me, it's true," he said. He had always liked it that way. He had always liked to go about in a jostling, happy crowd, the more loud and obnoxious the better. Back in his university days, he'd had the company of his best friends, Vincenzo, Rafael, and Jag. He sometimes thought those days in Oxford were a dream, because they had been the easiest of his life. Good friends. The time to hang about in pubs, heedless and young and magnificently rich.

But that was the trouble with a load of princes as best friends. They did, sooner or later, have to head back to their kingdoms to handle the responsibilities.

Even him.

And now he had a great many more people who liked to call him a friend, yet only the same three real ones. He'd replaced quality with quantity, and he could not say his life was richer for it. But it helped him play his part.

For the first time, he found himself wondering if it was worth it.

The question shook him.

"You're an interesting case," Nina said, looking at him as if to study him as they slid down Parisian streets and past iconic cafés. And Zeus shoved aside that odd feeling inside—because he'd made a vow. That made all this worth it, full stop. "You've never met a crowd you didn't like. And yet you wander around your own palace quite alone."

"The palace calls for gods, not courtiers, Nina. It's in the name. I can only obey."

"I'm almost tempted to suggest that everyone's favorite wicked prince has a public *and* private side. Yet you go to great lengths to pretend otherwise." He could feel her gaze on him. "Why?"

He sent a lazy look her way and tried not to think about the picture she presented. Sitting next to him in the back of a car, her long legs visible now and crossed at the ankles. The rest of her was almost dainty, small and narrow-shouldered, with a belly so big it shouldn't have been possible for such a small woman to walk around with it.

And yet she did. Seemingly without complaint.

Already the perfect mother, he thought.

And when the usual surge of something too much like emotion crested in him, he shoved it away again. The way he always did.

It was already bad enough that he'd mentioned his mother and started questioning the vow he had made over her grave. He could not start thinking of himself as a father. Or of his own father. Because everything he'd said about his mother was true. She had been a bright light in every respect. But she had been very young and too silly for Cronos, who had dimmed a little more of her light each day until it was extinguished.

And so, with his endless criticism and neglect, King Cronos had taken the only thing that mattered to his son.

Leaving Zeus to return the favor.

By making sure that the only things that mattered to Cronos—his throne, his pure Theosian blood, and the line of succession that would carry forth his bloodline into the future—would be publicly, repeatedly, comprehensively bruised. If not stained beyond redemption.

The truth was, Zeus had never planned to have an heir. He had gone to great lengths to ensure he could not possibly father one. But now, in his bitter old father's waning days, he would present the dying King with something even better than no heir.

An heir from a bloodline his father would despise, when there was nothing he could do about it.

He could not have planned it better if he'd tried.

When Zeus was out of Nina's presence, he thought the plan was divine. He had not intended to impregnate her, but he was delighted he had. Everything fell into place with this particular woman carrying the heir to the throne of Theosia.

It was only when he was with her and she aimed that secret, tender smile down at her belly, or when she spoke of things like her fears of motherhood, that he wondered what, exactly, he was doing.

But only for a moment.

Because Zeus had lost his soul long ago. When he was eleven, in fact, and his heart along with it. There was no getting them back now.

He told himself he hardly noticed the void.

His Parisian getaway was the two top stories of the quietly opulent hotel, far away from any other guests or nosy photographers. As soon as they arrived in the expansive suite, he had food brought in, because he knew by now that Nina was always hungry.

And as she sat in the living room and helped herself to the small yet epic tea provided, he welcomed in a smiling, diffident man with a briefcase connected to his body with a chain. Behind him came several more men, similarly attired.

They proceeded to set out their wares on one of the tables, and when they were done, they had set out the finest jewels that Europe had to offer.

"I don't understand what's happening," Nina muttered, but she was looking around with a sort of hunted look on her face.

"I suspect you do." Zeus went to take a seat next to her on the sofa she had chosen. He only smiled when she shot a fairly outraged look his way as his weight tipped her closer to him. He waved his hand at all the open briefcases, sparkling with rows upon rows of priceless, impossibly stunning rings. "Choose one."

Beside him, Nina simply…shut down.

"I wouldn't know where to begin," she said, and she sounded…different, somehow.

As if, unbowed by the entire house of Haught Montagne, and not too impressed with Zeus while she was at it, what had finally brought her to her knees was a private shopping expedition.

The woman was a revelation.

"If I may," said one of the men, looking closely at Nina. "I think I have just the thing."

He turned all the briefcases around and then did the choosing, presenting Nina with a selection of five rings instead of ten times the number. And every time she reacted, he switched the presentation until, at the end, only one remained.

And it was clear that no other ring could possibly have done.

It was lovely. Delicate, though it boasted a large, marquise-cut diamond set horizontally. It looked as if it had been designed for Nina's hand, so it nearly sang. Zeus watched as she looked down at it, an expression he couldn't read on her face.

Yet when the men had left, Nina pulled that beautiful ring off her finger and set it on the table before her with a decisive click.

"I can't wear that," she announced.

"Of course not," Zeus agreed, lazily. "I have yet to present it to you. On bended knee, very likely. It's a classic romantic gesture for a reason."

"No."

It registered on him that she actually seemed distressed, but before he could reach for her, she pushed herself off the couch and onto her feet.

"I can't wear that, Zeus. Look at my hands." And then, disconcertingly, she lifted her hands toward him, as if warding him off. "I spent ten years of my life scrubbing floors."

"No one will ask you to scrub floors while wearing a ten-carat ring, Nina."

"This whole thing is ridiculous," she threw at him. "No one will believe for one second that you're marrying a *servant*. A scandalous former servant. Because why would you?"

"I told you. This is a love story."

Because he needed it to be to really pour salt in his father's wounds.

That was what he kept telling himself.

She looked down at her bump. Then she lifted that same grave gaze to him. "No one will believe that, either," she said quietly. Yet with conviction—and he found he disliked it. Intensely. "I'm sure no one will have any trouble believing that I somehow fell in love with you, in my mercenary way, as gold diggers are wont to do. But anyone who has ever met you knows how impossible it is that you would ever fall in love with anyone."

Everything she said was true. And yet he wanted to argue—against the premise, against the names she called herself, against her description of him. Even though all of that was precisely why she was so perfect.

He opted to shrug instead. "And yet, why else would I marry if not for love?"

Nina only fixed him with that same look, much too grave for his liking. She stroked her belly. "I can't think of a single reason. Can you?"

She looked as if she was about to say something else, but then she squeaked a little. Her hands moved on her belly to press down, and because she was no longer wearing a tent, he could see the way her belly rippled.

When Nina looked at him again, her whole face was changed. Light. Shining.

And it hit him, suddenly, that when she wasn't wearing masks and pretending the way she'd had to do for so many years, this was what she looked like. Those brown eyes so bright they seemed shot through with sunshine. Her lovely face, open and happy. And that smile of hers, so charming that it lit up the whole of their hotel suite and likely outside as well, rendering Paris something other than gloomy this February day.

Rendering him...undone.

"Ouch," she said, but she was laughing. "Apparently our child would like to weigh in on this discussion. I'm almost certain it voted for no ring, no marriage, and no more of this silly game."

Zeus moved without thinking. He rose, moved to her, and then slid his own hands onto her warm belly. And he didn't so much hear the way she caught her breath. He felt it, as if she was inside him.

And he felt his child again.

He *felt*, and instead of shoving the feelings

away, he stood in them a moment. He kept his palms against her belly and felt her breath come faster. He let all of that wash around in him until he hardly knew who he was, and then he kept on.

"I don't think you're translating correctly," he said as he felt the little drumbeat kick beneath his hands. "The child clearly wishes his parents to marry. He's adamant."

"*She* thinks that she would be just fine as an independent entity," Nina replied.

She pushed his hands away, but then their hands were tangled up together. That wasn't any better.

Zeus wanted to laugh at himself, because if anyone had ever dared try to tell him that there would come a day that simply *touching hands* with a woman would so nearly destroy him, he would have laughed.

But everything with Nina seemed charged like this. One slip away from total detonation.

Little as he liked to recall it, it had always been like this. From that night in Haught Montagne when he'd pressed into a moment that had bloomed between them, thinking she would frown and dismiss him, but she'd laughed. It had seemed preordained.

This had always been impossible to resist.

If she hadn't disappeared so completely after that night, walking away from a castle with little more than a backpack, by all accounts, Zeus would have found her. He had tried.

He didn't like to admit how hard he'd tried. He didn't like to think of that strange autumn at all, when he'd been…not himself.

But he needed to remember his endgame. That was what he'd told himself then. That was what had to matter now.

He needed to keep his promise. He would.

For a moment he could see his mother's face, tipped back in that marvelous laughter of hers that had become so rare near the end. He had been so small, and she had danced with him, around and around to the music of the sun and the sea. He remembered how she'd swung him up into her arms and kept going, twirling until they were both dizzy.

Then they'd done it again.

And by the time Zeus had grown to a tall eleven, she didn't laugh any longer, and she certainly didn't dance, so it had taken coaxing for her to let him pick her up and spin her around in his arms, trying not to notice how frail she was. How tiny.

How destroyed.

Zeus let go of Nina's hands and stepped back. For a beat, he didn't know what he would do. Maybe run? Shout? He did neither. Though it hurt.

He smiled at the woman he would marry, and soon. To fulfill the destiny he'd made for himself not long after that day in his mother's chamber. Then he went and assumed his typical position on the couch, as if it had taxed him sorely to stand.

And he opted not to notice that Nina looked at him for much too long, her expression gone grave again, as if she could see straight through him.

When he knew no one could.

He'd made certain of that.

"Now," he said, with his usual dark humor, though it stung more today than it should have. It made his ribs feel dented. "Let me tell you how this will go."

CHAPTER SEVEN

NINA LEARNED A lot about Zeus over the following weeks.

When he mounted a campaign, he did not play around. He had made their hotel in Paris their home base, and she quickly realized why. Its little-used front entrance was on a busy street, but its back entrance was gated and equipped with a security officer. That meant that Zeus could decide when and if to play paparazzi games.

First he started telling his stories.

He did not get down on one knee. Instead, he slid the ring on her hand over breakfast their first morning there and told her to get used to wearing it. Then he called in what appeared to be the entire Parisian fashion world, paying Nina absolutely no mind when she protested, and insisted they use the front entrance.

"You must mean the back," she said when he ended the call. The ring was heavy on her hand. It dazzled her, catching her eye with its sparkle every time she breathed. The more she gazed at it, the more impossibly magical it seemed.

Even on a hand like hers.

"The more of a commotion out in front, the better," Zeus said. He offered her that wicked curve of his mouth. "Trust me, little hen."

"Well," Nina said, blinking at the blinding jewel on her finger. "That's very unlikely."

Zeus only laughed, low and hot, so that it rolled around inside her and made her feel shivery. Everywhere.

By the time they came, in a horde, Nina certainly wasn't *ready*. But at least she'd eaten and tried her best to get used to the idea.

Ten slender and severe-looking men and women, almost all in black, took over the suite's small ballroom. They wheeled in racks stuffed with fabrics and garments. They conferred with Zeus, pursing their lips and frowning at her, but then murmured appreciatively when they draped certain fabrics over her.

They did not appear to need *her* input at all.

"I don't need all of this," she complained, in the middle of the melee.

But Zeus only eyed her as if she was something adorable. Yet edible.

"I do," he said.

It wasn't as if Nina hadn't witnessed a fitting like this before. She'd sat through far too many of them, in fact. What she hadn't experienced, however, was a fitting like this in which she was the center of attention.

Gown after gown, fabric after fabric. Her measurements were taken, then retaken, while theatrical arguments in French swirled on all around her.

At one point, standing on a raised platform while a crowd of fashionistas revolved around her, she thought, *This is how a queen must feel*.

The ring on her hand seemed to buzz a little, as if it knew she'd actually dared to imagine herself in the role.

She sneaked a look at Zeus and found him watching her. He was leaning back against the far wall, another one of his dark suits looking as rumpled on him as ever. His ankles and arms were crossed, giving him the look of a sort of fallen angel.

But his green gaze was as hot as it was dark. And it was focused on her.

Nina flushed. And burned.

And yet she couldn't look away.

Almost as if she wanted him to see what he did to her.

When the fitting was finished, they left her with what seemed like an entire wardrobe that very same day. Yet promised to come back with what one stylish gentleman told her were *the important pieces*.

Nina both wanted and didn't want to know what those might be. Because she still couldn't quite accept that this was happening, maybe. Or because she and Zeus were left alone in a ballroom filled with racks of clothes. With no one else in this suite apart from his unobtrusive security detail.

He was still leaning against that wall. Like a taunt.

And all the things she felt, all the ways she burned, bubbled up inside her like a sob. She wanted to explode. She wanted to launch herself at him. She wanted—

"You must change into one of these new options," Zeus told her idly, though his gaze was still hot. Too hot. "You like art, do you not?"

She couldn't tell if she welcomed the shift in conversation or did not. And her cheeks were too pink either way.

"I question anyone who does not like art," she managed to reply.

"Then your task is to change into something appropriate for looking at art in Paris."

Nina lifted her chin. "Define *appropriate*."

He didn't smile, but his green eyes grew warm. He waved his usual languid hand, but this time at the racks of clothing.

But when she took too long, only staring at him like she couldn't quite comprehend anything that was happening—because she couldn't—he went and chose a few pieces himself.

Nina went up to the room he'd given her the night before, but she hardly saw it. She put on the simple dress he'd chosen, then sighed. Because it looked like nothing on the rack, but it fit her like a dream. The fabric was soft yet held enough of a shape that, once again, she could see the difference between her belly and her body.

And she blamed her hormonal state when she got a little teary at that.

She wrapped a bright scarf around her neck, knotting it carelessly, then pulled on the trench that slid over her shoulders like a hug. She looked in the mirror and thought it was all so beautiful that maybe, if she squinted, she was beautiful, too.

Just in case, she went and fixed her hair, too. And swept some mascara over her lashes.

When she came down the suite's winding stair, Zeus was waiting at the bottom. He took her hand and kissed the ring she wore, and she thought she wasn't the only one who felt shivery inside.

Then he led her to the nearest chair and helped her sit.

And she felt her mouth go dry when he knelt before her.

"I'm already wearing the ring," Nina managed to say. And she waved it at him, in case he'd forgotten in the twelve seconds since he'd kissed it.

"And it suits you," Zeus rumbled in reply. "But you will need shoes, I think, to brave the city."

Nina watched, then, as Prince Zeus of Theosia slid a delicate shoe, itself a near-operatic work of art, onto one of her feet. Then did the same with the other.

Like another prince she used to dream about. When she'd still believed in fairy tales.

She cleared her throat and reminded herself that these shoes, however stunning, were not made of glass. "I don't know if I can walk in these."

He pulled her up to stand in them, and she swayed, gripping him tighter.

"See?" she demanded. "It's a tragedy waiting to happen."

"Then lean on me, little hen," Zeus murmured, as she clung to him. "I promise, I will not let you or my child fall."

My child, she marveled. He'd actually said *my child*.

And the moment between them seemed dipped in gold. He stared at her for what felt like a millennium or two, then lifted her hand and the ring to his lips once more.

"You do understand that no one will believe this is real," Nina whispered, though she felt…fragile and beautiful, both not herself and more fully herself than before. "Since when have you wanted to do anything in private? Yet you supposedly proposed to the servant you knocked up where no one can see?"

"But of course." He lowered her hand and guided it to his arm. "This will only add to your mystery."

And that night, he took her on a private tour of several of Paris's most famous museums. She found that once she decided she could walk in her shoes, she did. And they were more comfortable than the heels she'd had to trot in while chasing Isabeau around. So comfortable she kept forgetting where she was, or who she was with, the better to tumble heedlessly into one masterpiece after another.

"What made you think to do this?" she asked at one point, her eyes almost overflowing with the marvels she'd seen tonight.

"The time you don't spend in the library you spend walking the halls, looking at the art on the walls and in the gallery," Zeus replied. Then smiled when her mouth dropped open. "I know. It is so difficult to imagine I could pay attention to such things, but I assure you, I do."

"Thank you," she managed to say. Awkwardly. But heartfelt all the same.

And he didn't look like himself then. No lazy smile, no laughing gaze. He only looked down at her as if they could have been anyone. Just a man and a woman in front of a painting so famous it had its own merchandise.

Just a man and a woman, a pretty ring, and the baby they'd made.

Deep inside Nina, a voice whispered… *what if?*

But his security detail entered the room, and the breathless moment was gone. And afterward, Zeus took her to a restaurant so exquisite that there was no name on its door, and when he ushered her inside, the maître d' nodded as if they were regulars, then greeted them both by name.

And it was later, much later, when Nina felt drunk on good food and great art. And, if she was being honest, the man beside her.

"I'd like to walk back," she said when the car pulled up before them on the narrow side street. "Either my feet don't hurt or they've gone completely numb."

"Very well," Zeus said and then looked behind her, doing something with his chin to alert his team.

Her hand still felt strange with the ring on

it, so she kept curling it into a fist and holding it up. As if, were she not careful, the ring would tip her sideways and take her tumbling down to the ground.

But then he solved the problem by taking that hand in his, and that was...

Nina told herself that she was drunk, even though she hadn't touched a sip of alcohol. She felt that giddy. As if she was graceful enough to turn cartwheels, walking down the street in the dark with a man so beautiful that every passerby who saw him stopped and looked twice.

And there were so many things she wanted to say to him, out here in these old streets. Points she needed to make, and then, while they were out here in the dark and the cold, perhaps a confession or two.

She was saved from all that, in the end.

Because by the time they arrived back at their hotel, a crowd had formed. Almost before she registered that all the people were waiting—and for them—the flashbulbs began popping.

It was as violent as it always was, and that was before they started shouting.

Her heart slammed against her ribs. She almost tripped over her own feet and was grateful she was holding on to Zeus for dear life as he pushed on through the wall of noise and disorienting bright lights.

It was a fight to make it into the hotel lobby, where it was mercifully hushed—but Nina could still hear all the shouting from outside. Zeus's security detail led them across the lobby until they reached the private elevator that brought them directly up to their rooms at last.

Nina was shaking. She didn't realize until they were inside their rooms with all the doors locked that Zeus was laughing.

Honest to God *laughing*.

"Why do you think it was funny?" she asked him, letting go of him to hold on tight to the nearest wall. She tried to reach down to take off her shoes, but she'd forgotten that her belly was in the way.

And she had to hold herself back from kicking him when he came over and knelt down to remove them. Just as she had to *not* punch him, hard, on his shoulder when she had the opportunity.

"You are shaking," Zeus said as he rose, his gaze narrow as it scanned her face.

"That was…" She shook her head. "I've been near scrums like that before, obviously. The last time they were shouting my name, I was half-asleep. This time I actually heard all the vile things they were saying about me. Or to me. I don't know how you can find it the least bit entertaining."

And somehow it felt right when he moved his hands to grip her shoulders. Gently enough, but they were still his hands. Holding her.

"Because that was all it took," he said, gazing down at her. "One evening out and here they are."

She could still hear the shouting in her ears. Her eyes were still dazzled by all the cameras. "Why do you want that?"

He looked confused—or whatever *confused* was on a man so convinced that if there was an answer worth giving, he already knew it. "We discussed this."

"We did not discuss it. You ranted on about telling stories and twisting narratives, but I didn't think…" But her voice trailed off.

"What, then, did you think it would entail?" he asked, his voice a gruff thread of sound. She didn't know why it sounded so loud when she'd heard real volume outside. And when she knew he wasn't shouting himself.

But all Nina could do was shake her head. "I don't know."

"Trust me." His hands gripped her a little tighter, then he let her go. And she remembered, suddenly, that bronze mask in the halls of his palace. He had never resembled it so much as he did now—and there was no trace of laughter on his face. "This is exactly what I wanted."

But that was the thing, she thought later, shut away in her room with the lights of Paris pouring in through the raindrops that coated her window, like the tears she refused to let herself cry. She did trust that all of this was what Zeus wanted. But how was she meant to trust that what he wanted was any good for her or the baby?

I don't believe he asked you to trust that, came a voice from inside her. *He only asked you to trust* him.

Nina curled herself up in a ball and tried to sleep, but when she did, her head was filled with images of Zeus on his knees, playing Cinderella games.

The headlines started pouring in the next morning.

And Nina quickly realized that Zeus did not intend to give any supposedly soul-baring interviews to carefully vetted, sympathetic journalists. That was one way of rehabilitating a reputation, though one rarely used to good effect by royalty. Instead, he made certain that he and Nina were seen out every night, taking in Paris like lovers.

To drive the point home, he doted on her. He held her hand as they walked. He was always leaning close when she spoke. He helped her into cars. He gazed into her eyes over dinner tables, smiled fondly when she spoke, and looked—in every photograph Nina saw of them—like a man besotted.

This strategy, he informed her with glee, allowed the tabloids and their readership to compare and contrast for themselves the difference between the arranged engagement to his Princess that he had clearly never wanted anything to do with, and the pregnant woman everyone now suggested he'd left Isabeau for. And would convince anyone who looked that the two of them were mad for each other.

He didn't need to announce any engagement, because the papers took care of that with their zoom lenses. The speculation about the ring she wore went on and on, and the more people carried on about it, the more Nina was described as not only the mercenary gold digger of yore, but something of a femme fatale besides. She was called a dangerous beauty, having hidden in plain sight for years before she'd taken her shot. Most agreed this was evidence that she was nothing but an evil whore. Still, others countered, her mix of innocence and beauty and a handy sob story made her the only one in all the world who could turn Prince Zeus's head.

Nina found it was less upsetting to read these stories about herself than she'd anticipated. Because it was still nothing more than a character she was playing to match the character Zeus was playing, wasn't it? It was no different than wearing her odd clothes and haphazard hair in a royal court.

Though every night she went to her bed alone and wondered just how much each one of them was playing.

By the middle of the second week, the stories were already changing. Who was this woman who had claimed the unclaimable Prince? Was she truly the disgrace of Haught Montagne, as advertised, or had the wicked Prince simply fallen in love with the lonely orphan girl? For how else was she able to succeed with Zeus?

She had to admit that the paparazzi were thorough in their research. There was a round of pictures she hadn't known anyone had taken, from a hostel she'd stayed at in Spain. But rather than creating a scandal out of the photographs of her at a party, the pictures made her into a different kind of heroine on the ravenous internet.

"Apparently I'm the introvert's mascot," Nina said from her favorite sofa, where she was enjoying another phenomenal tea. "It makes a change, as mascoting goes."

Zeus came over from whatever he was doing on his tablet and plucked the paper from her grasp, peering at the grainy pictures. "You look like a librarian shushing the obstreperous children."

"That's more or less what I was doing, if

memory serves." Nina shrugged. "Apparently I'm relatable."

"So my team tells me daily." He handed back the paper, his gaze as warm on hers as if they were out in public where photographers were always lurking. But they were in private. "You're making quite a splash. And not a hen in sight."

But the real test, Nina knew, was the upcoming ball.

At the end of their third week in Paris, they left France and headed to the tiny kingdom of Graciela, tucked away between France and Spain, where the country's newly crowned Queen was having a birthday ball. The expectation was that the guest list would be a who's who of European royalty.

"You look nervous," Zeus said with that lazy drawl that made it clear he was not.

Outside, Graciela was shrouded in clouds as Zeus's pilot circled the small airport, waiting for their turn to land.

"Not at all." Nina tried out a laugh that came out tinny. "Who doesn't love a bit of a swim, surrounded by so many sharks?"

"The trick is to pretend the sharks are minnows," Zeus told her, that green gaze of his a simmering fire even as he gave her that half smile. "And treat them like minnows. Most find it so confusing they spend the rest of the evening trailing about after you, begging for more."

"Sometimes," she said softly, "your cynicism about the human race is heartbreaking."

It was Zeus, so all he did was shrug. No matter how many times she thought she saw something else in those green eyes of his. She told herself it was the hormones They were making her see things that weren't there. And would never be there.

She had to stop looking at pictures of them in the tabloids and imagining what she saw was real, because she knew better.

Nina had to keep reminding herself that she knew better.

There was no what-if here.

"Whatever you do," Zeus told her, something darker in his gaze, "never show the sharks your heart, Nina."

She hoped she wasn't that hormonal.

Nina braced herself once they'd landed and were whisked to the royal castle, but she was surprised to find that the stuffy manners that she'd always found so tedious—mostly because it had been her job to use them in the wake of Isabeau, who did as she liked—were an excellent stand-in for the sorts of masks she used to wear. At first she wondered why it was that royal personages she'd met many times before were suddenly capable of being kind to her as they all lined up to be introduced into the ball.

"What a pleasure to meet you," said a queen here, a sheikh there, and excellencies everywhere. "Many congratulations on your most happy news."

Then she realized, it had nothing to do with her. It was all about Zeus.

Because he might be one of the biggest walking scandals in Europe, but he was still the Crown Prince of Theosia. And everybody knew that King Cronos was not doing well.

"They're already lining up to kiss your ring," Nina murmured as she and Zeus waited for their turn to be announced. Graciela's castle was, like all castles, all about its ramparts and keeps. The ball, thankfully, was being held in the new annex—which meant a grand covered gallery festooned with heat lamps and circulating attendants.

She wanted to laugh, maybe a little hysterically, at the fact that even the rulers and figureheads of Europe had to line up like so many partygoers outside a club.

"A kingdom is a kingdom, after all," Zeus told her, leaning down the way he did now. His mouth so close to her ear that goose bumps prickled down her neck. Or maybe that was because he had curled his hand over her nape. "Theosia might be small and unthreatening, and unlikely to wage war in the traditional sense, but there are always economic pressures that can be brought to bear."

"It's like you're a king already," Nina said with a sigh. She lifted a hand to rub at her neck, as if that could make the shivery sensation dissipate. It didn't. "Already plotting out your wars."

"You have not been paying attention." Zeus gazed down at her, unusually grave. "I've been at war my whole life."

She caught her breath, and her heart pounded—

But then they were being announced.

And she understood why he'd waited for this moment as they stood there at the top of a long stair. Because he had to do nothing but stand there, looking resplendent as ever in his formal attire. He looked even more impossibly beautiful than usual. And he had Nina on his arm, dressed in a gown so outrageous it had taken staff to help her into it.

This was the point all along, she understood as their names were called out and they started down toward the waiting crowd.

This was Zeus's engagement announcement. He'd planned it this way.

But when they reached the floor of the ballroom, he looked down at her and smiled as he took her by the hand.

And Nina…forgot. That all of this was planned. Plotted out ruthlessly by Zeus and his public relations people to create a story. This story. Just as he'd said.

She knew better than to believe any of it.

She knew better, but he tugged her straight out onto the dance floor, then pulled her into his arms. She knew better, but he gazed down at her…and suddenly it didn't matter what kingdom they were in, what ballroom. Who might be watching, or what the papers might say tomorrow.

There was only the way he held her, smiling down at her as he made the belly between them part of the dance instead of an impediment to it.

And Nina wanted fairy tales, the kind she'd dreamed of when she was a little girl.

She wanted all of them, she realized then, as she danced with her very own prince. She *wanted*, when she thought she'd gotten rid of that sort of thing long ago.

Because a girl who wanted in an orphanage was only destined for despair. And a girl who wanted anything at all in service to Isabeau would find nothing but pettiness and backstabbing.

Just like the girl who was foolish enough to have feelings for Prince Zeus was proving herself no kind of shark at all, but a minnow, through and through.

Nina knew all of that, and oh, did she know better. And still, as the music swelled and they danced around and around, she let herself pretend that this was real. That none of this was for show. That the way he looked at her meant what it should.

Tomorrow could do its worst. She had no doubt it would.

What if? she asked herself.

And tonight, she let herself believe.

CHAPTER EIGHT

NINA WAS SITTING at one of the tables set up in semiprivate alcoves dotted around the main ballroom. This part of Graciela Castle was clearly a more recent addition—meaning the last century or two—because each alcove was carefully situated with views out over the tiny kingdom's sweeping valley, covered in snow and dotted with light.

And to make the fairy-tale evening even better, she was waiting for Zeus to return with food. Because, apparently, in the role of Prince Charming that he was playing tonight, he not only danced with her...he fetched things for her.

It was all part of the fantasy she was letting herself believe tonight.

Nina took a deep, steadying breath and wondered if this was what it felt like to truly be happy. No expectations, no regrets. Just that look on Zeus's face and the fire that seemed to burn brighter between them by the hour.

She had no experience with happiness. The closest she'd come was out there on her brief travels—though even then, she'd still been so aware of what she'd run from.

Tonight she was only aware of Zeus.

And the way she felt when she was with him, the focus of all that bright green intensity.

Nina shivered a little, then laughed at herself. She patted her belly. *I think your father might be a good man*, she confided silently to her child. *When pressed. You'll see.*

The music was glorious, a full orchestra playing music to beat back the winter dark. And Nina almost felt as if she was a queen already, sitting here in sweet solitude as she waited for Zeus's return.

When she looked up and saw Isabeau descending upon her, her usual entourage fanned out behind her, her first thought was that she'd fallen asleep at her table and this was a dream. A dream she'd had more times than she could count. All of those haughty

and imperious faces, some already alight
with malice. If Nina had been with them, she
would have been shuffling along at the rear
of the pack, far enough back that she could
avoid the poisonous looks they liked to throw
her way.

Because they had gained their position with
Isabeau through the usual channels—that
being by the lucky accident of having noble
blood that stretched back through the ages in
Haught Montagne, as was proper. Nina had
wondered many times if her presence was an
insult to these other ladies-in-waiting even
more than to the Princess.

The way they were all glaring daggers at
her now, she had to assume the insult was
universal.

Princess Isabeau came to a stop before
Nina in a dramatic manner that she knew
very well made her skirt swirl about her while
showing her legs to best advantage. She prac-
ticed it. And it occurred to Nina that it felt a
lot like power to know the things she knew
about this woman and no longer have to hold
her tongue.

Not that she had to descend to Isabeau's
level. But she *could*.

"I can't believe you dare to show your face," the Princess said in her usual cutting tone. "Especially in your revolting state."

Nina understood that she was to take from that the clear message that her face was unpleasant, shown or unshown. Because Isabeau was a classically beautiful, tiny little brunette with a heart-shaped face and perfect bone structure, and she loved to make sure others knew how ugly they were in comparison. She particularly liked to let Nina know this.

It only occurred to her now that Isabeau would not have spent so much effort slapping Nina down about her looks—or her offensive lack thereof—if she hadn't felt threatened in some way. And why would she feel threatened? Only if Nina actually looked the way Zeus made her feel.

The revelation made her smile, far too brightly.

But "Pregnancy is quite natural" was all she said in return. "Some find it very beautiful."

And what a joy it was to say whatever she liked without having to second-guess her words or her tone or the expression on her face. She was no longer Isabeau's little pet.

Her pocket orphan that she could pull out whenever someone accused her of being exactly who she was as evidence that once upon a time, she'd had a benevolent impulse.

Nina couldn't seem to tamp down her smile, and Isabeau...actually looked uncertain for once. She brushed back a tendril of her lovely hair, her blue eyes narrowing.

Always a warning sign.

"Who do you think is buying this act? If Prince Zeus was capable of impregnating anyone, he would have had a parade of bastards by now." Isabeau sniffed, then looked crafty. Another red flag. But tonight Nina couldn't seem to work up the necessary concern. "The people of Theosia will rise up in revolt against a grubby commoner trying to pass off her baby as heir to their kingdom."

Nina had not seen that one coming. Maybe she should have. She laughed and took her time standing up from the table, propping one hand on the belly before her, big enough that Isabeau looked askance at it. "I assure you, Isabeau. There is absolutely no doubt about the paternity of this child."

And she wasn't sure she meant to, but she said that in such a steady, distinct way that there could be no doubt that she was announcing—in no uncertain terms—not only her relationship with Zeus but exactly how their baby had been made.

All right. Maybe she did mean to.

It felt…liberating.

Isabeau looked as shocked as if Nina had hauled off and slapped her. "You're nothing," she hissed. "You'll never be anything but a charity case. Don't you know that by now, Dumpy?"

Nina sighed. Not because the nickname hurt. It didn't. It never had. But it was only now that she'd stopped hiding herself that she realized how silly it was that she ever had. And how pathetic Isabeau was to issue taunts like they were on a playground.

That wasn't entirely true. She'd known it all along.

"We could have been friends," she said quietly. "Companionable, at the very least. Instead, you took every opportunity to prove how petty you are. I feel sorry for you."

Isabeau reared back. "*You* feel sorry for *me*? I am a *princess*. My father is a *king*."

"And so will my husband be," Nina replied coolly. "Making me a queen, yes? You will have to forgive me. I don't eat and sleep your hierarchies, but I believe I'll shortly outrank you."

Amazingly, the little coterie behind Isabeau actually…tittered.

Nina could feel everything change in that moment. Not because the courtiers had turned, the way courtiers always did. But because, at last, she truly felt free.

All this time, all the effort she'd spent, whether hiding from Isabeau or, periodically, attempting to placate her—all that was over now. And whatever happened next, she finally understood something she should have realized all along.

Her child would never find itself the plaything of a creature like this. Her child would never be lost. Her child would always know who and what it was. A prince or princess of Theosia. One day its King or Queen.

Nina had gotten lost after her parents died. But that would never happen again. Not to her and certainly not to her baby.

And once she understood that, how could anything else matter?

"I'm done with you," she said to Isabeau, then swept past her, thinking that she would head across the ballroom to search for food herself.

But she was brought up short to find Zeus standing there just outside the alcove with an expression she couldn't read on his face. Clearly having witnessed the entire interaction.

"Look at you," he said admiringly. He didn't say *little hen*, but it felt as if he had. "It appears you've found your claws."

Then he was looking past her and shifting where he stood, obliquely blocking her from Isabeau. Making his sentiments known.

Again.

"You're supposed to be with me!" Isabeau hissed at him. She stamped her foot. "Our fathers decided it. You can't possibly think you belong with that—that—"

"Princess," Zeus said, in the kind of quiet voice that made a wise person's hair stand on end, "I would advise you not to finish that sentence." He drew Nina closer, and if possible, looked even more like a bronze statue than ever before. When he spoke, his voice carried. "Nina is to be my wife. And, in due course, the Queen of Theosia. She belongs with me. Always."

And as declarations went, it was something. It was even more than *something* coming from him. Nina knew full well that some part of that statement would be on every tabloid around come morning. Maybe that was part of his plan. But she didn't care.

She belongs with me. Always.

Her whole life, Nina had wanted to *belong*. Of all the precious gifts this man had given her, this was the one that made her heart ache.

She didn't care if it was true. She cared that he'd said it.

Nina forgot all about Isabeau. She had the vague impression that her entourage herded her away, but she didn't bother to confirm it. She looked up at Zeus, and suddenly it was as if her belief in fairy tales had spilled over into…everything.

As if maybe it was all real. Complete with a vanquished villainess.

Because she felt powerful and beautiful. Their baby was safe and protected and always would be. And she had Zeus, looking at her as if she was magic.

She belongs with me.

"Remember when I told you not to kiss me?" she asked.

He looked devilish and amused at once. "I remember you spouting such nonsense, yes. I did us both a favor and ignored it."

"You haven't kissed me since."

"But if I'd wanted to, I would have," he said, all lazy drawl and a simmering heat in his beautiful eyes. "That's the key point."

"Zeus," she said. He looked down at her, lifting one marvelous brow. "Stop talking."

And then Cinderella lifted herself up on her tiptoes, leaned forward, and kissed Prince Charming herself.

Because it was *her* fairy tale.

He kissed her back with all the same heat. And then he pulled her with him, laughing, back to the dance floor.

"We cannot leave yet, my wild little hen," he told her. Sternly. "So we must dance."

But the moment they could leave without offending their hosts, he hurried her out of the ballroom and followed his waiting aide to the rooms set aside for them in Graciela's ancient castle.

"What is it?" he asked as they walked in, when Nina laughed. He shut the heavy door behind them and leaned against it.

Nina looked around. Stone walls, tapestries, and an old standing suit of armor in one corner. A fire crackling in an old fireplace. A weathered yet polished wardrobe. And thick, soft carpets thrown all over to mask the chill of all the stone.

"It's just…castles," she said, because it was somehow perfect that they were here, tonight. Making fairy tales real. "They are always the same."

She walked farther into the room, making her way over to the canopied bed that stood against one stout stone wall and running her fingers over the embroidered coverlet.

"Second thoughts?" Zeus asked, his voice a dark temptation, and she remembered that. He had asked that same question on their first night together, but then he had been poised above her.

The hardest part of him notched between her legs, the pleasure already unbearable— she remembered every moment.

She looked over her shoulder at him and smiled. "Not a one," she whispered.

And then she watched him come toward her, dark blond like one of the gods his people sometimes claimed his family had descended from. Green eyes that were darkly intent now and laced with that fire that was only and ever theirs.

He came toward her, then turned her in his arms, and Nina thought that surely now she would feel unwieldy again. Swollen and awkward.

But Zeus held her in his arms, he bent her back, and he kissed her.

Ravenously.

And Nina felt as light as air, as graceful as a dancer.

She met his kiss, all the fire within her bursting into spirals of flame that licked through her body, making her fight to get closer. To feel *more*. To glut herself on this man all over again.

He kissed her, and she kissed him, and it was different now. Better.

Laced through with a kind of reverence, as if neither one of them could believe that they were here again. In a castle, near a bed, just like last time. Nearly seven months gone by now, and it felt like yesterday.

"I looked for you," Zeus said against her lips. "You hid well, little hen."

"I wasn't hiding."

But then she was laughing as he lifted her

up as if she weighed no more than a feather and sat her down on the edge of the high bed. His hands were busy beneath her long skirts, and she sighed as he ran his palms up her legs, over her thighs. And sighed again when he only brushed, gently, the place where she needed him most. Then moved on.

She remembered this, too. That Zeus liked to tease.

"Were you not?" he murmured, trailing his fingers up the sides of her dress. "You were hard to find, then, for a person who was not hiding."

But he seemed distracted. He spent extra time on her belly, then found her breasts. Once again, only a glancing caress before he eased her back so he could attend to the complicated fastening of her gown down one side.

"I suppose I was running," she said, because this room felt like a confessional. This night felt like a brand-new start. "But I didn't know where I was going."

His hands stilled. "You only knew you wished to get away."

Nina smiled again. She couldn't stop smiling, really. She lifted a hand and slid it over his hard jaw, strong and solid. And, tonight, with that faint rasp against her palm that made all the fires he set within her kick a little higher. Burn a little hotter.

"Not from you," she said softly. "It never occurred to me that you would come looking. It was my one night with the wickedest, most notorious prince alive." She felt his lips curve as he turned his head so his mouth was against her palm. "That is the Prince Zeus promise, as far as I'm aware. One night. Never more."

"That is a very strict rule indeed." He pulled her dress away from her body and then left it open on either side of her, so she felt as if she was being presented to him on a platter of fine Parisian fabric. He moved so he was standing, positioned between her outspread legs. His gaze was a dark blaze as he looked at her, lying before him so wantonly with little more than a scrap of silk between her legs. "But it is for dastardly courtiers. Horrid princesses. Vapid celebrities of all stripes. Little hens are exempt."

Nina didn't feel like a hen, she felt like his, and perhaps that was the same thing.

She pushed herself up on her elbows, watching him greedily as he slowly, deliberately, set about ridding himself of his own clothes. Slowly, with that half smile on his face, he stripped himself down and tossed his discarded garments toward the cases his servants had set up. Then he was standing before her, naked.

Far more beautiful out of his clothes than in them.

Zeus came down beside her on the bed. She could feel his sculpted chest against her as she turned toward him, and once again, his mouth found hers.

And for a while there was only that slick heat, that mad spin. As potent as the first kiss. As irresistible as the last.

But he pulled away and directed his attention lower. He concentrated on her breasts first, gazing at them in wonder.

"You astound me," he whispered in a rough voice, his green eyes nearly black with desire.

Then he used his mouth and his tongue, even the scrape of his teeth. His big, hard hands. Every trick at his disposal to coax her into wave after wave of impossible sensation. It raced from his mouth straight down between her legs and had her moaning.

Nina hadn't known how much more sensitive she was now.

But Zeus did.

And he took his time, showing her all the ways her body had changed.

She began to move her hips, pressing herself against his hard thigh, there between her legs.

And he laughed, the way she remembered him laughing before. That sound of dark, endless delight.

It made her burn all the more.

Outside, the snow came down, but in this room the fire that crackled in the grate was no match for the heat between them. Nina couldn't think what could be.

Zeus worked his way down her body, so slowly she wanted to cry. Maybe she did. And finally he found her belly and laid kisses behind him, everywhere he touched.

Something in her seemed to glow almost bright enough to hurt. That there could be all this heat, all this mad, greedy desire, and yet in the middle of it, a tenderness. Affection. She was making love to a father, not just a man.

This was no fairy tale she'd ever heard of. This was hers, and it was theirs.

And it was real.

But then he wiped all those thoughts away when he moved even lower, crawling off the side of the bed so he could pull her hips to his face.

His mouth closed over the mound of her softness, and she jolted, even though he had yet to remove her panties.

This was only a test. A temptation. And it still punched through her, a lightning bolt of pure sensation.

Nina made a sound that was neither a sob nor a scream, but somehow both. She lifted up her hips, begging him mutely.

Zeus laughed again.

Then he tugged her panties from her hips, peeling them off her with exquisite slowness. Down one leg, then the next, taking his time.

Only then did he move back into position. He gripped her hips with his strong hands, tilting her toward him. And then licked his way into the very center of her heat.

And this was not the waves of sensation from before. This was a thunderstorm. A whole hard crash.

Nina shattered at the first lick and then never quite came down again.

Zeus, naturally, settled in. He took his time.

And wanting him was nothing new, but Nina knew she had not been this sensitive before. That every time he breathed, her body reacted like this. With a greedy, encompassing joy that she couldn't have contained if she'd tried.

It felt like a gift.

She was limp and sobbing when he finally rose up. He looked down at her like that bronze mask, passion making his features almost stern. If it weren't for that glittering heat in his green eyes, she might have found him frightening.

But she could see how much he wanted her. Looking at the hard jut of his sex made her flush hot all over again.

Zeus pulled her legs around his waist, then angled himself down onto the bed. He propped himself up on one arm and gazed down at her. His chest was moving like hers, like breathing was hard. His gaze was possessive. Commanding.

And all she wanted to do was melt against him, then ask for more.

He gripped his sex with his free hand and guided himself to her entrance. Then he stroked her there, with that hardest part of him that felt to her like bronze.

For a moment their eyes met, and the blaze of intensity there almost sent her over the edge again.

Almost—but then he thrust inside, filling her completely at last.

At last.

Nina could no longer tell if she was at the edge or over it, so intense were the sensations, so wild was this fire.

She gripped his arms as he moved over her, setting a slow, deliriously intense pace.

A rhythm she could feel everywhere, inside and out.

And the dance had been a fairy tale, but this was something better. She didn't think it was hormones any longer, not when her chest ached the way it did and every stroke seemed to open her up more inside. Her heart. Her poor heart.

But it was worth breaking if she could have this.

He dropped his head to pull one nipple into his mouth, hard enough that the electric jolt of it seemed to travel straight down her body into the place where they were joined. And once again, she was sent hurtling.

Hurtling and hurtling, and she heard him shout out her name as he followed.

He flooded her, and she cried out as she shook and shook.

It wasn't until she'd recovered herself some little bit that she realized what she'd said. The secret she'd been carrying all along.

"I love you," she had told him, again and again. "I love you, Zeus."

And she was terribly afraid she'd ruined everything.

CHAPTER NINE

HER WORDS ECHOED inside of him like doom.

Or grace, whispered a voice within.

Zeus had almost forgotten himself, and that never happened. But the taste of her had exploded through him. She had rocked him. He had found no defenses when usually he was the king of them.

The kiss in the ballroom had nearly undone him. He, who had spent his life chasing every sensation available, had nearly been brought to his knees by this woman. In the middle of a ballroom, with the eyes of the world upon them.

And he wasn't sure he would have cared.

Zeus had never cared about making a scene. On the contrary, he went out of his way to cause as many as possible. But he could not bear the idea of further exposing Nina to the same censure.

He'd already done that.

And he, who regretted nothing, had regretted the scene he'd set up in Haught Montagne ever since.

But he shoved those things aside. The rest of the evening had passed in a blur, of faces and names he knew he ought to know, because she'd kissed him. Nina had dismissed the Princess who had caused her so much trouble with a wave of her hand. Then she'd looked around, every inch the perfect queen, and smiled when she'd seen him.

Then Nina had kissed him.

Entirely of her own volition.

With all that melting, glorious heat.

There could be no concerns that he had seduced her this time. There were no worries that he was exerting pressure on her in any way. Zeus would have sworn to anyone who asked that such things did not concern him— so confident was he of his appeal—but Nina was different.

She had been different that night, and he hadn't been prepared for it.

And now she was the mother of his unborn

child. She wore his ring. And she had kissed him like she was the one who'd chosen him from the first.

It was as if that kiss had woken up a part of him he had come to believe no longer existed. Or had never existed. She had chosen him, and she made him believe that he might have a soul after all.

And, more unimaginable still, a heart.

He had felt it pound in him, like it was pounding out her name.

Then they had come to this room of stone and fire, high up in yet another castle filled with so many of the same people doing the same tedious things, and once again, she had humbled him.

She had done it that first night. She did it with ease. She made him new, scrubbed him raw, and he didn't like it. He told himself he *couldn't* like it.

He didn't know what to do with it.

So Zeus had done the only thing he could. He had closed the distance between them, the hunger in him a wild and uncontrollable roar, and he had taken her in his arms at last.

Here, where there were no witnesses. No paparazzi and none on call. There was no press release, no story. No narrative to tinker with.

There was just this beautiful woman who was only his, who had danced with him tonight as if he was a dream come true.

He wanted to be that for her in every possible way.

And then, finally, he'd placed her on the bed and taken her the way he'd begun to imagine he never would again.

It had felt sacred.

Like a vow.

Like a simple, honest truth, stark and irrevocable.

And when she cried out those words she should have known were forbidden, Zeus couldn't bring himself to react the way he knew he should. Instead, he moved them both up in the bed, then pulled the coverlet over them so they could lie there, together.

Because he needed to gaze at her as if he expected, at any moment, that she would be taken from him again. And that, once again, it would be his fault.

"We never talk about that night," he managed to say. His eyes were so greedy on hers, he felt so torn, that he was surprised she could stand to hold his gaze at all. But she did.

"What is there to talk about?" He thought that was a slap, a dismissal. Instead, Nina rolled closer to him and piled her hands beneath her face so she could smile at him. It felt like a miracle. *Maybe she is the miracle*, something in him whispered. "We both know what it was between us. How intense it was. What it meant. Yet it was always going to end the way it did. Because you'd already called them."

The last time she'd mentioned this, he'd deflected. *Were you truly under the impression that I was or am a good man?* And maybe he would never be a good man. Not by any reasonable measure.

But for Nina, he would try.

"I did," he said. Simply enough.

And of all the things he'd done in his life. All the sins, all the scandals. They seemed like nothing to him. It was this admission that cost him the most.

But her smile didn't waver. *I love you*, she'd said. And unlike the many who had mouthed those words before, she knew him.

She'd seen him do more than flatter and cajole a night away.

She'd chosen him, not his reputation.

"Zeus," Nina said quietly, her brown eyes soft. "I understand."

Then she leaned toward him, kissing him again. And it was as if she'd flung open the windows and let the noonday sun inside. He felt that light all over him. He felt bathed in sunshine.

He knew that if he bothered to look, it would still be dark outside. A cold winter's night, with snow coming down as if it might never stop, up here in the mountains.

And Zeus had spent his entire life, it seemed, finding new ways to be worse. To be even more terrible than reported. To live down to every low expectation his father had ever set him.

He'd come to think that the reason it came so easily to him was because that was who he was. That all along, he hadn't been acting at all.

But the way Nina looked at him, as if he was the miracle here, made him feel something he had long been certain he would never feel again.

Hope.

"You shouldn't understand," he told her fiercely, his hand going to her so he could grip her, to make sure she was real. "You should hate me. Why don't you hate me?"

"I've tried," she admitted, with that smile of hers. "Believe me, I did try. But it turns out, I don't know how."

What could Zeus do but kiss her again then, with all those things he thought he'd lost. His soul. His heart. Himself.

And he knew that morning would come. As morning always did. He knew that his endgame marched closer every day, regardless of what work he put into selling the world love stories. It would all come full circle soon. He was ready.

But here, now, far away in this castle room where no one could see who they truly were with each other, he let himself be the one thing he'd never been. In all his years of pretending to be this or that. Or everything.

Here with Nina, his Nina, he let himself be nothing more or less than a man.

Not just any man, but the one she loved.

Again and again.

There was a faint hint of light in the sky

outside when Zeus woke again to find Nina curled up next to him. The sight caught at him, hard enough to leave marks. This woman who gave all of herself to him, when she, more than any other, should never have let him near her again. That big, round belly where his child grew, safe and warm. He kissed them both. Nina on her cheek, so she smiled a little while she slept. And his baby, too.

His baby. Zeus hadn't let himself truly take in what that meant. That in only a couple of months, he would be able to hold a child of his own in his arms.

He would be able to do it differently. To do it better.

Take what had been done to him, but turn it inside out.

The heart he'd just rediscovered seemed to crack open inside of his chest. He tried to imagine Nina in the role of his mother. Or himself a king like Cronos. He tried to imagine letting all of that weight land on the tiny life inside Nina's belly, and he couldn't. It was too much. He wanted to rage. He wanted to punch the stone walls surrounding him.

He wanted to go back and change everything. Save his mother. Save himself.

And somehow find a way to keep his father from walking the path that had led them here.

Maybe what he couldn't accept—what he'd never been able to accept—was that, given the chance, he'd save his father, too.

He didn't want to feel these things. He didn't want to *feel*. He had always chosen to see himself as a finely honed weapon of a particular vengeance. Nothing less, nothing more. As he had vowed over his mother's grave he would become, so he had done.

Yes, yes, such a weapon, his friend Vin, more commonly known these days as His Royal Majesty, the King of Arista, had said with an eye roll when they'd all gotten together for a drink in Paris.

Perhaps the weapon has grown a bit blunt now that you're impregnating women and parading them about Paris with statement jewelry, Prince Jahangir Hassan Umar Al Hayat had murmured, lounging in the chair opposite in the private club. Jag had grinned. *I recall a time when all you could do was extol the virtues of prophylactics*.

Rafael Navarro, bastard child of the former King of Santa Castelia and long its regent, had laughed. Vin had joined him. Zeus, who knew exactly why they were laughing, forced himself to smile when he would really rather...not.

There are a great many virtues in impregnating the wrong woman and making her a wife, Rafael had said. As he would, having recently scandalized the whole world by kidnapping his own woman from her wedding to another man. Another man who had happened to be Rafael's half brother. *I recommend it.*

I second this recommendation, Vin had said, sounding revoltingly happy.

I have no intention of settling like the two of you, Jag had said, shaking his head at them. *I prefer the time-honored practice of not making my lovers accidentally pregnant.*

His friends and he often cleared their schedules and made drinks happen in various cities, all these years after Oxford. Zeus had been surprised at how little he had wished to leave Nina in their hotel for even so short a time. He, who had never turned down the opportunity for a social event in all his days.

Particularly not when it was with these men. His closest friends.

His only friends.

But he had only shrugged languidly, as if he was still the same *him* he had ever been. *I believe you are all mistaking the matter. I salute your fecundity, truly. Yet I assure you—my situation is not emotional, however accidental. It fits in nicely with my plan or I would not have moved forward with a wedding. Have you met me? Do I seem the marrying kind?*

And he had pretended not to notice how Vin and Rafael had looked at each other then.

He couldn't seem to get that look out of his head now.

Because the way his friends had gazed at each other had seemed ripe with a kind of emotion Zeus would have sworn neither of them could feel.

Yet maybe what he'd been worried about after all was what *he* felt.

What he had always felt.

Zeus kept circling back to the fact that whatever the shape of the weapon he'd made himself into, that hadn't been what he'd wanted. It had never been what he'd wanted.

He'd gone to great lengths to deny it, but at heart, he'd wanted what any child did. His mother. His father. His family.

And it only occurred to him now—here in this room with a woman who had knocked him off balance from the start—that maybe it wasn't the vow that he'd made at his mother's grave that had motivated him all this time. Not entirely.

Maybe it was the longing of a child, after all.

Zeus told himself he was horrified at his own mawkish sentimentality.

He made sure Nina was covered as he left the bed. He moved over to the fire, pulling the quilt that they'd long since kicked off around his waist. And then he sat, stared into the flames as they danced before him, and, for the life of him, could not understand how things had come to this point without him realizing what he was doing.

Not his own feelings, which he assured himself he could dismiss as he should have long ago. But to *her*. To his Nina. For a man was no man at all who hurt the woman he should protect. Hadn't he learned that when he was young? In the worst possible way? He knew he had. It had changed the course of his life. It had made him who he was.

How could he possibly justify using the woman who loved him, despite what he'd done to her, as a pawn in this bitter game?

The fire gave no answers.

Zeus kept imagining holding his baby for the first time. Staring down into the eyes of his own child. And it was so powerful that it threatened the favorite image he'd been carrying around for more than half his life now. Of staring down at his father on his deathbed, diminished and humbled, and making sure the old man knew that despite everything, Zeus had won.

It was like the two things were at war, ceding no territory.

Tearing him apart.

"You look cold," came her voice, so soft it cut right through him. "Are you all right?"

And Zeus had no idea how to answer that.

Nina was beside him in the next moment, kneeling down with him on the thick, priceless rug before the fire. She drew the coverlet with her, wrapping it around the both of them while she slid her legs beneath the quilt.

He thought she would ask questions, but

she didn't. She only sat with him, her thigh against his, until he shifted her so he could hold her before him. She sat between his legs and leaned back, resting her head against his shoulder.

Even then, she only gazed into the fire. As if she knew that simply sitting with him soothed him, somehow. It was as if the heat of her body was hope itself, curling its way into him whether he wanted it there or not.

Whether he wanted to believe in it or not.

He rested his chin on the top of her head. He wrapped his arms around her.

It was only then, in a room dark save for the fire, that he found himself able to talk.

"They say my mother died of heart failure," he told her, amazed at how easily the words came after so long spent holding them in. And letting them poison him. "And in the end, she did. But it was more complicated than that."

"I'm so sorry," Nina murmured.

Somehow that made him want to go on rather than stop, when he would have said he was allergic to pity.

"I told you what a joy she was, but there were many others who did not think so. My father chief among them." He heard Nina murmur something and held her tighter. "I cannot say when I began to understand that the way my father spoke to her made something in her die a little. He was so much older, you see. She had been given to him after his first Queen died, taking his hopes of extending his bloodline with her. That was what he cared about. Bloodlines. The throne. The kingdom. What he did not care about was his young, silly second wife, who he took on purely to breed an heir."

"Maybe he didn't know how to care about anything but those things," Nina said softly. "Do you know what his relationship was like with his first wife?"

That walloped Zeus. Hard. Because in all this time, across all these years and all the bitter hours he had spent cataloging his father's many sins, it had never occurred to him to think of such a thing. He knew about the Queen who had come before his mother. He knew her name and some part of her story. But he'd been so focused on the wrong that had been done to his mother that he had never asked too many questions about the woman who had preceded her.

"I always assumed she suffered the same fate," he said.

"But you don't know?" Nina sighed a little. "Maybe he loved her. And hated that he couldn't have her but felt he needed to have a child."

"Nina." Oddly enough, he wanted to laugh. "Do not defend him."

"I'm not defending him," she replied. "It's not his heart I'm worried about."

His own heart kicked at him unpleasantly. But he kept going. "My mother was soft. It was part of what made her sweet, but she was no match for life at court. The courtiers and sycophants took their cues from my father, and she wasn't like you. She didn't know how to hide herself away. She didn't know how to protect who she was inside. And each harsh word, each bit of malice, each laugh at her expense took more and more from her."

Zeus couldn't remember now why he'd started to tell her this story. But as she nestled in closer against him, something in him eased. Or made room, maybe, so that he could keep going.

"First she would harm herself," he said. "Bruises. Cuts. Not where anyone could see when she was in public. But I saw." He shook his head. "Over time, it became clear that she wasn't eating. That every time someone criticized her, she punished herself for her flaws by taking away food. And then, I suppose, it was not so much a punishment any longer, but how she made her point. How she got the last word."

"Zeus…" Nina whispered.

"They tried to intervene. But in the end, I suppose it was the one place she could assert her will, so she did. And eventually, her heart gave out."

He heard her whisper his name again. He felt the touch of her lips at the side of his neck.

And he had never told anyone this story before. It was the only story that mattered, and he peddled his stories to anyone who would run with them, but he never gave them this one. Maybe it was that Nina knew tragedy, too. Or maybe it was that she was Nina. And the simple fact of her, sitting here and bearing witness to this tale, made it better.

Not what had happened. But how it sat in him, even now.

"I was eleven years old." Zeus pulled in a

breath. "And I was the one who sat with her at the last. And in my rage and grief, that day and into her funeral, I made a vow. I promised her as she was laid to rest that I would keep it."

Nina slid her hand over his chest. It took him a moment to realize she'd put her hand over his heart. He covered it with his.

"It was my father who could have helped her. Who, if not the King? Her husband? He could have stopped what was happening. He could have thrown out anyone who dared speak ill of her. He could have stopped criticizing her himself. There were any number of things he could have done, but he didn't." Zeus heard that roughness in his voice. He knew it told too many truths about him— more than he liked to share. Perhaps even with himself. "I vowed that I would ruin the one thing that mattered to him."

He heard her quick, indrawn breath, though Nina said nothing. But she didn't have to.

"Yes," he said. "I made it my mission in life to tarnish the throne. So that the Throne of Ages would find itself polluted by the most disreputable, irresponsible, unworthy occupant of all time."

That wasn't all of it. But it was enough. Zeus's heart was still jarring against his ribs. He felt outside himself, and that was before Nina turned to kneel before him so she could meet his gaze.

"I know that's the role you play," she said quietly. "But is that really you?"

Something swelled at him, so sharp he assumed it must have been bitterness—though he worried it was something much worse. *Hope*, something whispered in him. "Do you not know? And this the man you claim to love?"

But if he imagined she might look away, or be shamed in some fashion, he was disappointed. She only gazed at him as steadily as before.

"I know what I believe," Nina said with that quiet conviction that made him ache. "The question is, what do you believe?"

There was a roaring in him then. On and on it went. And her gaze was on him, in him. And he *felt*. He felt…everything.

This woman had haunted him for seven months now, and she haunted him still. And Zeus understood then that it was entirely likely she always would.

Still, that storm raged on inside him. Still, the roar of it was loud enough to blow this stone castle to ash.

Zeus did the only thing he could think of to do.

He bent his head to hers, taking her mouth in a kiss that said all the things he could not. All the things he would not.

Everything he wished he could say to her. Only and ever to her.

Over and over again, he kissed her.

And he moved within her there, before the fire, until the shuddering took them both. Sweet this time, and more dangerous for it. Then he lifted her up, carried her to the bed, and took her once again.

Hot and hard.

As if in the taking, the sweet glory of this maddening fire, he would find the answer. What he believed. What he wanted. Who he was.

And in the meantime, he would hold her like sunshine between his hands and warm himself until hope felt as real as she did.

They had fallen asleep again when a great pounding came at the door.

Zeus rose, pulling on his discarded trousers as he stalked to the door. He flung it open to find the better part of his guard standing outside.

"Your Royal Highness," said the head of his security detail, bowing his head. "I'm afraid there is news of the King. His condition is grave."

For a split second, Zeus thought he had missed it—but no. There were rituals for that. His guard would have knelt. They would have called him *sire*.

He could see from their expressions that they would do these things. Soon.

"How long?" he asked curtly.

"A matter of hours," the man replied.

Zeus nodded, then closed the door. He turned to find Nina watching him, and he braced himself for her reaction. She would fly to him. Offer condolences that he would reject. Try to comfort him, and it might send him into a rage.

But she only gazed at him with what he was terribly afraid was compassion.

"I will find my things and dress," she said.

All Zeus could do was nod. All he wanted to do was reach for her. Turn back time, live in this night forever.

But his father was dying. It was time to go home.

And, whether he liked it or not, honor the vow he'd made so long ago.

CHAPTER TEN

THE FLIGHT BACK to the island was terrifying at first, as the pilot fought the winter weather to get them aloft. But once out of the mountains, everything was smooth. And, to Nina's mind, almost frighteningly quiet the rest of the way until they landed in the bright sun and soft breezes of Theosia.

The moment they returned to the palace, Zeus stalked away, surrounded by his aides. And looking more alone than she had ever seen him.

Nina found herself left to her own devices. Standing in the middle of a palace that was now hushed in dreadful anticipation.

And she'd spent her life mourning her parents' deaths. She had no idea how a person *prepared* for such a thing.

She walked, not sure where she was

headed, in and out of the glossy, exquisite rooms that seemed to glisten with their own history. And it was perhaps unsurprising that she eventually found her way into the gallery of family portraits. The Kings and Queens of Theosia, stretching back into antiquity.

Nina looked at all of them, starting as far back in time as the pictures reached. Slowly, slowly she advanced through the ages until she found her way to the small collection of portraits on the farthest, emptiest wall.

She recognized Zeus immediately. Only a small child in the painting, but undeniably him. The same green eyes. A smile made more of mischief than of studied wickedness, but his all the same. His hair more blond than dark, and the hint of all that austere bronze yet to come.

Then she studied the painting of King Cronos, who she had never met. He had been too ill the whole time she was here. Yet she could see Zeus in the face of the proud man she gazed at now, dressed in all his finery. The same forbidding features. The same hard, sensual mouth.

Beside them hung two very different portraits. One was of a dark-haired woman with eyes of violet and a reserved curve to her lips. Next to her hung a young blonde with emerald eyes and the biggest smile yet in this room full of portraits.

And Nina's heart hurt.

For all of them. But mostly for Zeus. For the little boy with such a big name in the portrait in front of her and the man she'd sat with so early this morning, feeling the clatter of his heart against her back. Hearing each and every betraying scratch in his voice.

She didn't know how long she stood there before she gradually became aware that she wasn't alone. When she turned to look, she saw Thaddeus, Zeus's sniffy butler who had so disdained her on sight.

"Madam," he intoned by way of greeting.

Nina sighed. Maybe it was time for more sad antechambers. "Have you come to encourage me to leave the portrait gallery to my betters?"

But even as she asked the question, she saw that his gaze was on the portrait of Cronos's first Queen, not on her.

"Did you know her?" she asked.

Thaddeus looked surprised for a moment, then something like resigned. He put his hands behind his back and stood taller. "Which 'her' do you mean?"

Nina looked back at the portraits. The reserve in one, the irrepressible life in the other. And the portrait of the King, looking young and mighty. "Either one of them."

"It was my very great honor to have served them both in some small capacity," Thaddeus replied in reliably frosty tones.

Nina smiled at him. Winningly, she hoped. "What were they like?"

"Madam. Of all days, this day cannot be the appropriate—" He stopped himself, but not until Nina had seen what looked like genuine emotion in his gaze. He looked down at once. "I beg your pardon."

"One day my portrait will hang on this wall," Nina said quietly, looking at all the space on this white wall. And trying to imagine her contribution to this long line of people who didn't seem like people any longer, not once they were captured in oil and framed. "And I would hope that if anyone asked, you or someone like you would tell them who I was."

Thaddeus drew himself up. "I would never dream of attempting such an impertinence."

"I'm sure I'll look suitably grand, like everyone else," Nina said, looking over at the rest of the gallery. "But a portrait can't show the truth of things. That I showed up at the palace gates six months pregnant with snacks in my purse. My hair in a mess, and no apparent decency at all. Wouldn't it be a shame if there was no one here to tell *that* story, Thaddeus?"

If she wasn't mistaken, she saw the faintest hint of a thaw in the old man's bearing. Only a hint.

But eventually, the butler cleared his throat and indicated the first Queen.

"Queen Zaria was a childhood friend of His Royal Majesty," Thaddeus said. "They grew up together here on the island and were promised to each other when they were very young. No more than five, as I understand it, and from that time they were always together. By the time they married, it was very clear that they were not only great friends, but very much in love."

Love stories, Nina thought, her heart clutching in her chest. They always ended badly. It was only fairy tales that ended well. *How do people survive these love stories?*

How was she planning to survive the one she was currently living, for that matter? She looked down at her ring, adjusting the way it sat on her finger, and admitted to herself that she just didn't know. Maybe she wouldn't. Not in one piece.

Last night had made it clear that she was all in here, in the very last place she should ever have risked herself. But there was no taking it back.

Nina acknowledged that she wouldn't take it back if she could.

Thaddeus was still speaking, his gaze on Queen Zaria. "They tried for many years to have an heir, with no success. It is my understanding that they were finally successful, but something went wrong. Both the Queen and the unborn heir were lost."

Nina found she had her hands on her own unborn child. "That's a terrible story."

"Look around," Thaddeus invited her. "Look at all the people who hang here. More often than not, they are all terrible stories. Crowns and palaces do not protect anyone. Not from life."

And she couldn't tell if that was pointed or simply true.

"What of the second Queen?" Nina asked.

Beside her, Thaddeus seemed to grow more grave. "The King mourned for some time. Years passed, but he felt he had a duty to his people. Queen Stevi was from a noble, aristocratic family. She had been raised to marry a man of stature. She was innocent but not unprepared." He blew out a breath. "The papers love to pretend otherwise."

"The papers love to pretend," Nina agreed.

The butler bowed his head slightly. Then continued. "The palace had become…dark. It was a place of grieving, with no place for the brightness of youth. The Queen produced an heir quickly and was soundly praised. But it is my understanding that once the task was accomplished, it was felt that she had very little to offer."

And Nina could hear all the court gossip behind those words. All the pain and misery. It was not hard to imagine a bright, happy girl gradually reduced to one more tragedy in a place like this. All the white walls and sunlight in the world couldn't make a toxic environment better. It only made it shine.

Is this really what you want? she asked herself. *For you or your baby?*

But there was a different king then, she reminded herself. A different king than the one who would ascend soon. A different king. Not hers.

"And the King?" she said now, her voice small. She almost didn't dare ask. "Does he yet live?"

"His Royal Majesty clings to life, madam," Thaddeus said. "But barely."

"And Prince Zeus?"

"Has only now left his side."

They both stood there a while longer, staring at the same four portraits, until something dawned on Nina. She turned to look at the crusty old man, standing beside her looking deeply aggrieved he was here.

"Did you come to find me?" she asked. "On the Prince's behalf?"

"Not on his behalf, madam. No."

But Nina understood. She smiled, so wide she made herself laugh. "That does make a change, doesn't it? You tracking me down and then wanting to take me to the Prince. Who could have guessed, all those weeks ago in that musty little antechamber?"

Thaddeus only inclined his head. He looked as if he smelled something rotten.

But Nina felt warm inside. Because she knew, somehow, that this was the beginning of a beautiful friendship. She almost said so, just to see him sneer again without actually sneering.

He didn't lead her to Zeus so much as he walked out of the palace, headed into the extensive grounds, and wound his way down to a secluded cove. Where he left her at the top of a set of stairs with a significant look.

Nina padded down the stone steps cut into the hillside and found Zeus at the bottom.

He was still dressed in the clothes he'd thrown on back in Graciela. He stood and stared out at the sea. Perhaps wishing it would turn stormy and turbulent instead of its offensive deep blue and calm turquoise.

She walked across the sand, then stood by his side, and waited.

"He sleeps," Zeus gritted out.

"Did you speak to him at all?"

Zeus did not move, and yet Nina felt as if he was turning deeper into stone as he stood there. "It is not certain he will wake again."

She remembered asking him about loneliness that night so many months ago. Because she knew her way around it, having had little company but her own her whole life, no matter how many people were around. Much like him, she supposed, if for very different reasons.

But she had never seen anyone more lonely than Prince Zeus now.

It was not lost on her that her declaration of love had not exactly gone down well. Nina had been surprised by it herself. She'd never said those words to another person, not as long as she could remember. She already whispered them to her baby. But they had simply poured out of her mouth last night.

Because somewhere between the ballroom and the bedroom, she had come to understand that it wasn't make-believe with Zeus. It wasn't stories told, or publicity stunts. Not for her. Once they looked at each other, really looked at each other, in Haught Montagne that night, everything that came after had been inevitable.

It felt good to finally admit it.

She had loved him then. She loved him still. And the baby growing ever larger within her was simply one more manifestation of that love. Nina couldn't wait to see who their child would become.

And these seven months of pregnancy had taught her something else, too. It wasn't necessary to know every last detail about a person to love them. It was not even required that love make rational sense. Sometimes it was a look. A quickening. An instant understanding of life forever altered.

Her life was altered. There was no denying it.

She wouldn't take that back, either.

Nina moved closer and took his hand, there before the water that the Theosians beckoned daily, even in these less godlike times. And when he looked down at her, somewhere between shock and astonishment, she squeezed his fingers harder in hers.

"I love you," she said.

And Zeus seemed to shatter, even as she watched. He gritted his teeth so hard she saw the hard cords of his neck stand out. She felt his hands clench, though he did not grip her hard enough to hurt.

"Do you know what I plan to say to my father should he regain consciousness again?" he growled, his voice gone raw.

But Nina did not let go of his hand.

"I've been planning it since you came here.

It is the crowning achievement of my lifetime of disappointing the man." His hand flexed in hers. "And it is all because of you."

He turned to face her, so Nina took his other hand. He stared down at where they were linked and made a low noise, like an animal in a trap.

But he didn't pull away.

"I have all the pictures to show him," Zeus gritted out. "Every scandalous paparazzi shot from the summer, to refresh his recollection. He was apoplectic when it happened. And I've been biding my time, waiting for his final moments to tell him that it is all much worse than he could imagine. Much worse than some pictures in the papers."

She could see that he wanted her to say something, but she couldn't find the words.

"I have been looking forward to this," Zeus continued. "To telling him I'm marrying a commoner, a nobody. An orphan girl who was cast aside by her own country but bears the heir to the throne he loves so much. It will be a masterstroke."

Nina wasn't sure, then, if she felt relief or a hollow sort of despair. Relief, because she'd known that all of this had to be a game. She'd known all along. And little as she minded Isabeau's taunts and gibes, name-calling and spitefulness, she found she minded much more that this was how Zeus truly saw her.

Even if he looked like it tormented him.

But beneath that, that sense of despair. Because she believed he was a better man. The man she'd seen in snippets, here and there. The glimpses she'd seen of him in what looked like the sort of meetings no one would believe the notorious Prince Zeus could sit through, much less command. The man who had slid shoes on her feet so gently and had stood just outside that alcove so that she might handle her former life on her own. The man who could have found her a few gowns for his pictures but had ordered her a queen's wardrobe instead, and who took an obvious delight in dressing her. The man who not only told her she was beautiful but made her feel it.

The man who made love to her like it was a sacred ritual, burning them both clean and new.

She believed all of these things fully. And it felt like a kind of agony that he did not.

"If you wish to say all these things to your

father, why are you here?" she asked quietly. "Down on the beach, where if he stirs, it might very well take you too long to race to his side so you can hurt him one more time."

Nina could see the storms in his eyes. The glaze of grief. "You don't understand."

"I do," she replied calmly, though she felt anything but inside. "You saw me choose not to take my revenge on Isabeau. It would have been easy enough to do. It doesn't occur to her yet that I know all her secrets, but it will. I get to take pleasure in not sinking to her level."

He pulled his hands from hers, but he didn't stalk away as she half thought he might. He only stood there, letting the wind move over him while his green eyes were like thunder.

"It is hardly the same thing."

"It doesn't have to be the same thing. I still understand. That's called empathy—but I know they don't teach much of it in prince school."

"Nina."

The broken way he said her name pulled at her, but she pushed on anyway. "I learned some things about your father today. That he loved his first wife. Probably all of his life. And that she died, taking his unborn heir with him."

"Everybody knows this story," Zeus gritted out. "I learned it as a child."

"But you are only paying attention to the *story*, Zeus. I want to talk to you about a man." Nina shook her head when he began to speak again. "To you, he's larger than life. Your father. Your King. The man you blame—and possibly rightly—for making your mother's life so very difficult. All I am asking you to remember is that at the end of the day, he's just a person. And people are complicated. Good and bad. Kind and vicious. They can be all things. And your mother died so young herself, when you were just a child. It's only natural that you hated the person you felt was responsible."

"Because he is responsible. He could have stopped it." He looked ravaged then, but he sounded worse. "He could have *helped* her."

Nina went and took his hand again. She held it between hers, close to her heart.

"Do you have any idea what I would give for a single hour with my father?" she asked, holding his gaze no matter that the look in his eyes was painful. "With either one of my parents? I spent a lifetime wishing I could have another moment. Just one more moment, just enough, so I could tell them the only thing that really matters."

He said something, and she thought it was her name, but the wind stole it away.

"That I love them," Nina whispered. "That I will always love them. That no matter what happened to me, no matter what the years without them were like, I could never let that be what little I have of them. I would regret it forever."

He shook his head, as if warding her off.

"Zeus," she said, low and urgent. "Don't do something you'll regret forever."

"And what if I'm not the man you think I am at all?" he demanded, bringing his face in close, torn apart with emotion. No bronze mask. Just…him. All of him. "What if I am, instead, the creature I have always played? No regrets. No compassion. No love. What then, Nina?"

She reached up so she could hold his beloved face between her hands. And she gazed up at him, only dimly aware of the tears that wet her cheeks.

"Then I will regret it all for you," she promised him. "Your commoner queen, who will love you anyway, no matter how little you love yourself."

And for a moment, he only stood there, as if caught in his own storm. Nina thought she heard the ominous roll of thunder.

Then, as if it caused him physical pain, he pulled away from her. He staggered back, his green gaze locked on hers.

It felt like a lifetime.

But then Zeus turned away and left her behind on that beach.

Nina wrapped her arms around their baby, promised it all the love neither she nor Zeus had known, and stayed there.

Until her tears were gone.

CHAPTER ELEVEN

KING CRONOS WOKE in the evening, and Zeus was there. The nurses made him comfortable, fluffing his pillows until he frowned and waved them away. Then they left father and son alone in the King's traditional bedchamber.

Zeus had always hated this room. Everything was too martial, too imposing. All about history and tradition. He preferred sunlight and space to all this heaviness.

But he had never thought to ask *which* history his father was mired in. He had always assumed it was all Theosian history and had never cared for the yoke of it himself. But now he wondered if these stout furnishings reminded the old man of something else. Something personal.

Someone.

He didn't ask now. He stood against the nearest wall and gazed down at what age had done to the man he recalled as far mightier than the sun. The true god in this palace dedicated to them.

Back when he had been so small and useless.

Nina's voice sounded in his head. *He's just a person.*

Zeus could admit that he had never thought so.

"I did not think I would see you again," Cronos rasped. And did not look as if he was best pleased to see Zeus now.

Because even at a moment like this, he knew how to provoke his son. Zeus reminded himself that he had not become who he was out of nothing.

"I've been waiting for this moment," he drawled, lounging against the wall in the indolent way that he knew had enraged his father since he was little more than a sulky youth. "Surely you know that. A most indecorous deathwatch, I think all your acolytes would agree."

Cronos only laughed, though it sent him into that rattling cough that had slowly taken him over this last year. "Such is the weight of the crown, my boy. You must wait for the moment of my death to rise. And you cannot mourn for even a moment. You must rule."

Zeus wanted to launch into one of his diatribes. He'd been practicing them for years. He had looked forward to this moment with all that he was. Before Nina, he had planned to vow, here on the old man's deathbed, that he would never have a child. That he would make sure the throne passed out of this family forever, so that all the old man's machinations had been for nothing.

With Nina, he'd thought he'd have an even better knife to stick in, deep.

Because he could still remember sitting with his mother as she slowly faded away, that little smile on her face. So pleased that she had, in her death, done one thing to please herself completely. He could remember every moment of her last days.

He had been holding them close ever since. Hoarding them so he could build his fury about what had happened, year by year.

But now he was in another room in this palace, at another bedside, and yet his head was still back on that beach. *I will love you anyway, no matter how little you love yourself,* she had said.

And Zeus found he could not bring himself to say the things he should.

"Do you believe I will mourn you, old man?" he asked, almost idly.

And for a moment, he saw again the canny, shrewd King who had ruled his country long and well, through wars and plagues and famines alike.

"It is all mourning, in the end." That gaze of his still packed the same punch. "Remember that, Zeus. If you have any stake in this life at all, sooner or later, you mourn."

And maybe that was the word for what tore Zeus apart. Maybe it was all mourning, after all. For what he'd lost. For what he'd found but had intended to betray in this way. Maybe that made sense of the heaviness in him and the heart he'd only just discovered, broken into pieces.

And all of that wrapped up in an eleven-year-old's rage and grief for the mother who might not have left him if anyone beside him had loved her.

He cleared his throat. "I planned to send you off into the afterlife with the knowledge that I have not only impregnated Princess Isabeau's scandalous orphan, but I will also be marrying her in short order. Forever tarnishing your throne, your reputation, and therefore all you hold dear."

Cronos stared for a moment, and Zeus expected him to start in with the usual outrage. But he didn't feel even remotely as entertained as he'd always thought he would. He felt no rush of glee. No cleansing rush of spiteful triumph.

And it had never crossed his mind that he might find his revenge…underwhelming.

His father began to laugh again, though it made him hack and sputter. It took him a long time to catch his breath again. For a moment, he looked as if he might slip back into sleep. Instead, he roused himself, and when he looked at Zeus again, it was with an expression Zeus had never seen before.

As if his father was almost…bittersweet.

It had his throat tightening up.

"There is no throne in this world that is not tarnished," Cronos said. "It is only that, once the tarnishing has occurred, we all rally about and claim it as gold."

Zeus's pulse picked up then, though he was

still. Very still. "And here I thought the only thing that mattered to you in this world was that throne."

"Because it was all I had," Cronos blurted out, as if the words had been tamped down inside him a long while. And the saying of them seemed to exhaust him. He collapsed against his bed, his breath coming harder. But he kept on, looking determined. "I lost everything. The throne was all that remained. And it took me too long to understand that a throne is nothing but a bloody chair. What matters is who sits upon it—and what he does when he is there."

They held each other's gaze for what seemed like forever. Zeus knew that these were words his father never would have said if these were not, perhaps, his final moments. But then, he knew that he would not have listened otherwise. And as they gazed at each other without rancor for the first time in more years than he cared to count, Zeus felt as if a thousand more unsaid things passed between them.

"Father," Zeus began.

The old man lifted a trembling hand. "You have nothing to apologize for, my son," he said, still holding Zeus's gaze. "It is the regret of my life that I did not see what I was doing to your mother, so lost in my own misery was I. And that I remained lost for far too long. I want you to know that if I could, I would go back and change what happened. I would change…" He broke off and smiled, faintly, though his eyes were sad. And his voice was fading. "I would change everything."

And then Zeus found himself doing something he would have sworn he would never, ever do.

He went and sat by his father's bedside. He took the old man's hands and looked deep into his eyes. Because he had stood on a beach and told Nina what kind of man he was, and she had loved him anyway. He knew the power of it.

And how could he deny it to his father now? When he knew how it had felt to hear Nina say those words to him?

I am sorry, Mother, he said inside. *I have been choosing you for a lifetime. But this is the end of his.*

A moment he had been waiting for, thinking he would taint it with revenge. But now he was here, and it was happening, and he couldn't find the will to do it.

He had chosen bitterness his whole life. What would happen if he chose peace?

If he let himself love his father a little, too?

"Father," he managed to say, though his voice was raw. "Rest now. I love you."

And when Cronos's eyes closed again, there were tears on his creased face.

Zeus did not know how long he sat there, but he thought it no more than a handful of minutes. And then his father breathed his last.

And Zeus did not move.

His heart was racing, his ribs too tight. And he knew that he only had a moment left. He only had a single, solitary moment left. One final moment when he was a son sitting beside his father. One last moment when he was who he had always been. Prince Zeus of Theosia.

Not a good man, perhaps. But he had great plans for his future.

First, however, he would step out of these doors and everything would change.

But then, everything had already changed. He was to be a father. There was a woman who looked at him as if he was worthy of her.

She did not need him to save her. She wanted only for him to love her.

"I wish we had done it better," he said to his father, in this last moment that was only theirs. "I wish we'd changed everything together."

He set the old man's hand down. And then he sat back and thought of his mother. His laughing, lovely mother. He was older now than she'd been then. And he had his own child on the way.

So he whispered the words he'd never thought he'd ever utter, not to her. "I forgive you, Mama."

For leaving him. For, in her way, taking him on as harrowing a journey as his father had.

Because in the end, both of them had been too locked in their own misery to care for their child as they should have. He understood that now.

But he did not intend that history should repeat itself. His child would know exactly how much it was loved. Always.

Zeus gave himself one last moment in his chair. Then he rose and blew out a breath. He looked at his father one last time as a son. Then he turned and opened the door.

He had stepped through it a prince. He would exit a king.

And he swore he would do a better job with the new title than he had with the old.

But as his father's attendants rushed inside, he didn't stand there and wait for them all to drop to their knees and "Long live the King" him the way tradition dictated they should. He was moving, rushing through the palace, because he was already King. It didn't matter who acknowledged it.

What mattered was her. Nina.

She was not in her rooms.

She wasn't in the library or any of the galleries.

Zeus was heading back to the beach when he finally found her standing in one of the palace's main halls, contemplating a large bronze mask.

And a thousand things he needed to say stormed within him. He wanted to tell her everything that had happened. Everything he'd understood, almost too late. Everything said and unsaid.

She turned as she sensed him coming, or

perhaps he made some noise, and he knew she could see what had happened. Right there on his face. He expected her to call him *Your Majesty*. He expected her to curtsy. He expected that, like every other person in this palace, she would look to his rank first.

He should have known better.

"Oh, no," said his Nina. His perfect little hen. "*Zeus*. Your father. I'm so sorry."

She opened her arms wide, and he moved into them. And then, somewhere in that mess of grief old and new, there was still Nina, and he was kissing her—the heat undeniable.

But all of these other things as well.

And so it was that the brand-new King of Theosia knelt before his scandalous orphan in a hallway where anyone could see them. He wrapped his arms around her.

"Nina," he said, very solemnly. "I love you."

She was crying, and he would have to do something about that, but she was smiling, too.

"I suspect I am very bad at it," he continued. "But I think, if I try, I will figure out how to love you as well as I pretended to disdain everything else."

"Just love me," Nina whispered. "Love us. Everything else is negotiable."

He stayed where he was, his face against her belly, hugging his child and his woman at once.

And when he rose, he wiped away her tears. Then he reached down and retrieved the ring he'd put on her finger. This time, he held her hand while he held the ring up between them.

She was still smiling, though her eyes were still wet. "You already did this, Zeus."

"I did not. Not properly."

"But—"

He lifted her hand to his lips, and she subsided.

"Nina, I love you," he said again, because it could never be said enough. "As I have told you before, I could command you to marry me. But I would rather you do it because you wish to."

And this was harder. So much harder than he'd imagined. Nina was gazing at him, her eyes damp and filled with all the things she'd taught him. Love. Hope.

Forgiveness not because it was deserved or earned, but because it was necessary.

"The King of Theosia will need a queen," he managed to get out past that tightness in his throat, "but I need you. My people will expect me to fail, for that is what I've taught them I do. But you expect me to fly, Nina. And I think that the better I love you, the easier it will be to spread our wings. And I already know that a man is only as good as a woman who imagines him better."

"It has always been yes, Zeus," she whispered. "It will always be yes."

"And in return for these services to man and crown," he continued, though there was light in him now, beating back the shadows. Sunlight, at last. "I will take all the time and energy that I have dedicated to my foolish plans and leverage them on you instead. We will raise our child together, and we will be happy, Nina. If I have anything to say about it, and I do. *We will be happy.*"

"We will be us," Nina said, moving closer so she could reach up to pull his face to hers. She kissed him then. His forehead. His jaw. "Not our histories. Not what happened to us. Not the things we did before we found each other. We will be you and me and the family we make together. We will be *us*, Zeus."

"Forever," he vowed.

And the hall was getting crowded. There were matters of state to attend to—and there could be no more putting off this moment.

Zeus slid that ring back onto Nina's finger, where it belonged. And when she took his hand and held it tightly, all he saw was sunlight. He felt it, deep inside.

I will do it right this time, he told his parents. *I promise.*

"We'll do it together," Nina whispered, as if she'd heard.

And then, hand in hand, they turned to face the future.

The way they always would.

CHAPTER TWELVE

THE FUNERAL PROCESSION took over most of the island. The citizens of Theosia came out in force to mark the passing of their King, whose reign had been long and stable.

They were less sure about their new King.

But a week after his father was laid to rest, Zeus married Nina at last. They stood together in the island's cathedral and spoke all the old words to each other. And new ones that were only theirs. That was the day he made her his Queen, though the coronation would come later.

Not without telling a few stories along the way. The papers were filled with all kinds of theories about the fall of wicked Prince Zeus—and how, perhaps, the most unlikely bride was the only one who could civilize the savage beast.

"This is utter nonsense," Nina complained, sitting with him at the table in his morning room, the light he loved so much making her blond hair gleam like gold. Her brown eyes danced. "You were never a *savage* beast."

Zeus took that as a challenge. And by the time he was done, she was limp and smiling in the vast bed in the rooms they now shared—his rooms. Neither one of them wanted to move into the King's traditional chambers.

They both wanted that light.

As much of it as possible.

"Your friends have all made a point of telling me that they're disappointed you didn't officiate your own wedding," Nina said at the grand reception after their wedding.

Zeus looked over the press of well-wishers who'd crowded into the palace and saw Jag, Rafael, and Vincenzo standing together. They all lifted their glasses in a mocking toast. He inclined his head in return and reminded himself that he was a king now. He could summon his best friends and call it a treaty summit. He made a mental note to do just that.

"Pay them no mind," he told his wife.

"They are shocking reprobates, every one of them."

She made a face at him. "No wonder you all get along."

He and Nina danced and danced. And every day, she was lovelier to him. But perhaps never lovelier than she was then, wearing her stunning white dress, round with his child, and beaming with happiness.

Later that night, they stood on their balcony, looking out over the island that had always been his and was now hers, too. There were fireworks going off in all the villages, celebrating the kingdom's new start.

And what it represented.

Hope.

"You're mine first," he told her, standing behind her as he had so many times—so he could put his arms around her and hold both her and their future close. "But from this day, you're also Theosia's. You belong to us all now, Nina."

He wasn't surprised to find tears on her cheeks again, even as she smiled with all her might.

"I will do you all proud," she promised.

But Zeus was already proud.

Their son was born late, prompting idle speculation in all the usual places that the new Prince intended to take after his father. And maybe he would one day. But first, there in the palace with the medical staff standing by, he was a miracle.

Maybe an everyday miracle, but a miracle all the same.

Zeus held the tiny bundle with wonder and awe and looked down at the perfect little boy who he knew would take after his mother. If he had anything to say about it.

And they loved each other as best they could, year after year. Wholly. Fiercely. They didn't always see eye to eye, but they fought hard to get back there. Every time.

The commoner Queen of Theosia gave the kingdom not only an heir but three spares. And they loved her for it. She made her royal children work with their hands as much as possible and treated any hint of laziness as a violent illness that required immediate attention. She insisted on kindness. She applauded thoughtfulness. She also loved them all to distraction, made them all feel adored, and was, without contest, the heart and soul of the family. And so, too, in time, the kingdom.

Her passion was orphanages and lost children of any kind, and she became a patron of too many struggling organizations to count—at home and abroad.

Princess Isabeau of Haught Montagne, when reached for comment about her once-fiancé and the orphan girl she'd taken into her court so benevolently, never had a thing to say except that she wished them every happiness.

Not in public, anyway.

For his part, Zeus tried to learn from the first part of his life. He tried to love more. He worked hard at being good at all three of his important roles. Husband. Father. King. He hid himself less and less and found it more amusing than anything else how surprised people were to discover that in private, he'd been an excellent prince all along.

He took his stewardship of Theosia seriously but ruled with compassion.

He loved his children. He delighted in them.

But most of all, he loved his wife.

"Are you lonely?" she asked on their wedding anniversary, some twenty years into their beautiful future.

"Never," he replied at once, holding her in

his arms in that very same Parisian hideaway where he'd first put his ring on her finger.

"That's a good thing," she replied, turning in his arms and wrapping herself around him with the same bright, hot passion that only grew between them. "But even if you were, I know the cure."

Because she healed him, the way she always did. And over time, he found ways to return the favor. Mostly by loving her so much and so hard that she never again doubted he always would.

"This is our fairy tale," he told her. "We make the rules, little hen."

"Fairy tales end happily," she liked to tell him as he swept her into his arms. "That's the most important part."

Zeus had to say he agreed.

And that was how a common, possibly scandalous orphan—from nowhere with nothing—married the wickedest, most notorious prince in all the land.

Then tamed him. Just like that.

* * * * *

If you were blown away by
The Scandal That Made Her His Queen,
*you're sure to love the first and second
installments in the
Pregnant Princesses quartet*

Crowned for His Christmas Baby
by Maisey Yates
Pregnant by the Wrong Prince
by Jackie Ashenden
*Don't forget to come back for the final
installment in the series,*
His Bride with Two Royal Secrets
by Marcella Bell

*In the meantime, don't miss out on these other
Caitlin Crews stories*

Chosen for His Desert Throne
The Secret That Can't Be Hidden
Her Deal with the Greek Devil
The Sicilian's Forgotten Wife
The Bride He Stole for Christmas

Available now!